Two Women

From the Mss. of Dr. Leonard Benary

Henry Harland

Alpha Editions

This edition published in 2024

ISBN : 9789362928658

Design and Setting By
Alpha Editions
www.alphaedis.com
Email - info@alphaedis.com

Contents

CHAPTER I.
THE FIRST NIGHT.

My name is Leonard Benary—rather a foreign-sounding name, though I am a pure-blooded Englishman. I reside at No. 63, Riverview Road, in the American city of Adironda, though I was born in Devonshire. And I am a physician and surgeon, though retired from active practice. My age can be computed when I say that I came into the world on the 21st day of July, in the year 1818.

I must at the outset crave the reader's indulgence for two things. First, my style. I am not a literary man; and my style will therefore be ungraceful. Secondly, my provincialisms. I have lived in Adironda for very nearly half a century, and I have therefore fallen into divers local peculiarities of speech. But I have a singular, and I believe an interesting and significant, story to tell, and I think it had better be ill told than not told at all.

It begins with the night of Friday, June 13th, 1884.

Towards twelve o'clock on that night I was walking in an easterly direction along the south side of Washington Street, between Myrtle Avenue and Riverview Road, on my way home from a concert which I had attended at the Academy of Music. Moving in the same direction, on the same side of the street, and leading me by something like a hundred feet, I could make out the figure of a woman. Except for us two, the neighbourhood appeared to be deserted.

Anything about my fellow pedestrian, beyond her sex, which was proclaimed by the outline of her gown as she passed under a street-lamp—whether she was young or old, white or black, a lady or a beggar—I was unable, owing to the darkness of the night, and to the distance that separated us, to distinguish. Indeed, I should most likely have paid no attention whatever to her, for I was busy with my own thoughts, had I not happened to notice that when she readied the corner of Riverview Road, instead of turning into that thoroughfare, she proceeded to the terrace at the foot of Washington Street, and immediately disappeared down the stone staircase which leads thence to the water's edge.

This action at once struck me as odd, and put an end to my pre-occupation.

What could a solitary woman want at the brink of the Yellow Snake River at twelve o'clock midnight?

Her errand could scarcely be a benign one; and the conjecture that suicide might possibly be its object, instantly, of course, arose in my mind.

My duty under the circumstances, anyhow, seemed plain—to keep an eye upon her, and hold myself in readiness to interfere, if needful.

After a moment's deliberation, I, too, descended the stone stairs.

CHAPTER II.
AT THE RIVER SIDE.

Yet to keep an eye upon her was more easily said than done. At the bottom of the terrace it was impenetrably dark. Not a star shone from the clouded sky. The points of light along the opposite shore—and here and there, upon the bosom of the stream, the red or green lantern of a vessel—punctured the darkness without relieving it. Strain my eyesight as I might, I could see nothing beyond the length of my arm.

But the lapping of the waves upon the strand, and about the piles of the little T-shaped landing-stage that extends into the river at this point, was distinctly audible, and served to guide me. Towards the landing-stage I cautiously advanced; and when I felt the planking of it beneath my feet, I halted. The whereabouts of the woman I had no means of determining. "However," thought I, "if her business be self-destruction, she has not yet transacted it, for I have heard no splash."

Ah! Suddenly a flare of heat-lightning on the eastern horizon illuminated the land and the water. It was very brief, but it lasted long enough for me to take my bearings, and to discern the object of my quest.

She was standing, a mass of shadow, at the very verge of the little wharf, distant not more than three yards in front of me. A moment later I had silently gained her side, stretched out my hand, and laid firm hold upon her by the arm.

In great and entirely natural terror, she started back: as luck would have it, not in the direction of the water, for else she had certainly tumbled in, perhaps dragging me with her. And though she uttered no articulate sound, she caught her breath in a sharp spasmodic gasp, and I could feel her tremble violently under my touch.

I sought to reassure her.

"Do not be alarmed," I said, speaking as gently as I could; "I mean you no manner of evil. I saw you come down here from the street above; and it struck me as hardly a safe place for a person of your sex to visit alone at such an hour."

She made no answer. A prolonged shudder swept over her, and she drew a deep long sigh.

"You have no reason to fear me," I continued. "I have only come to you for the purpose of protecting you, of being of service to you, if I can. Look—ah! no; it's too dark for you to see me. But I am a white-haired old man, the last person in the world you need be afraid of. You would not tremble and draw away like that, if you could know how far I am from wishing you anything but good."

She spoke. "Then release my arm."

Her tone was haughty and indignant. She enunciated each syllable with frigid preciseness. From the correctness of her accent and the cultivated quality of her voice, I learned that I had to do with a woman of education and refinement.

"Then release my arm."

"No," I said, "I dare not release your arm."

"Dare not!" echoed she, in the same indignant tone, to which now was added an inflection of perplexity. Sightless as the darkness rendered me, I could have wagered that she raised her eyebrows and curled her lip.

"I dare not," I repeated.

"Possibly you will be good enough to explain what it is you fear."

"Frankly, I fear that you mean to do yourself a mischief. I dare not let go my hold upon you, lest you might take advantage of your liberty to throw yourself into the water."

"Well, and if I should?"

"That would be a very foolish thing to do."

"But what concern is it of yours? What right have you to molest me? My life is my own, is it not, to dispose of as I please?"

"That is a very difficult and subtle question, involving the first principles of theology and ethics. I do not think we can profitably enter into a discussion of it just now, and here. But this much I will promise you," said I, "I shall not let go my hold upon your arm until I am persuaded that you have renounced your suicidal purpose."

She gave a *tchk* of exasperation. Then, after a momentary silence—

"You are insolent and intrusive, sir. You presume upon the fact that I am a woman and alone, to take a shameful and unmanly advantage of me."

"I am sorry if such is your opinion of me," I returned. "I do only what I must."

"You tell me you are an old man. I am not old, and I am strong. I warn you now to let me go. I assure you, you are unwise to trifle with me. I am a very desperate woman, and shall not mind consequences. If you try me beyond endurance—if we should come to a struggle——"

"Ah! but we will not," I hastily interposed. "You will not improve your superior strength against one who is moved by no other feeling than goodwill toward you. And besides," I added, "though it is true that I am close upon sixty-six years of age, my muscles have still some iron in them. I fancy I should be able to hold my own."

This, I must acknowledge, was sheer braggadocio. I weigh but nine stone, measure but five feet four in my boots, and am anything rather than an athlete.

"You are a meddler, sir. Good or bad, your motives do not interest me. Let me go. My patience is exhausted. I will brook no further interference. Release my arm. Your conduct is an outrage."

She spoke in genuine anger, stamping her foot, and tugging to escape my grasp.

"What I do, madam, be it outrageous or otherwise, I am in common humanity bound to do. I should be virtually your murderer if I did less. It is my bounden duty to restrain you, to do what I may to help you."

"Help me, sir? You are in no position to help me. I have not asked your help. There is no help for me. You are meddlesome and officious. I will not dispute with you further. *Let me go!*"

She spoke the last three words with threatening emphasis. I could hear her teeth come together with a decisive click after them. Again she tugged to break loose from me.

"You require of me the impossible," was my reply. "It is impossible for me to let you go. I implore you to control your anger, and to listen to me for one moment. You are labouring under great excitement, you are not accountable, you are not yourself. How can I let you go? I should never know another instant of peace if I stood by and suffered you to do yourself the injury that you contemplate. I should be a brute, a craven, a criminal, if I did that. I should be answerable for your death. As a human being, I am compelled to restrain you if I can. You must see that it is impossible for me to let you go."

"Well, have you finished?" she demanded, as I paused.

"Not quite," I answered, "for now I must ask you to let me take you to your home. Tomorrow morning you will feel differently, you will see all things by a different light. You will thank me then for what you now call an outrage. Think of your friends, your family. No matter what anguish you may be suffering, no matter to what desperate straits your affairs may be arrived, you have no right to attempt your life. Besides, you say you are young. Therefore you have the future before you; you have hope. I am older than you, and wiser. Be advised and guided by me. Come, let me take you to your home."

"Home!" she repeated bitterly. "Home, friends, family! Ha-ha-ha!" She laughed; but her laughter was dry and sardonic, horrid to hear. "What you say would be cruel, sir, if it were not so highly humorous. You speak and act in ignorance. You are very far from comprehending the situation. I have no home. I have no family, no friends, and, worst of all, no money. There is not a roof in this city—no, nor in the whole world, for that matter—under which I can seek a welcome; not a friend, acquaintance, relation, not a human being, in short, to miss me, or even to enquire after me, if I disappear. Except, indeed, enemies; except those who would wish to find me for my further hurt: of them there are plenty. Now will you let me go? I am in extreme misery, sir. There is no help for me, no hope. My life is a wreck, a horror. I can't bear it, I can't endure it any longer. Let me go. If you understood the circumstances, you would not detain me. If you knew what I am, what I have done, and what I should have to look forward to if I lived; if you knew what it is to reach that pass where life means nothing for you but fire in the heart: you would not refuse to let me go. You could condemn me to no agony, sir, worse than to have to live. To live is to remember; and so long as I remember I shall be in torment. Even to sleep brings me no relief, for when I sleep I dream. Oh, for mercy's sake, let me go! Go yourself. Go away, and leave me here. You will not repent it. You may always recall it as an act of kindness. I believe you mean to be kind. Be really kind, and do not interfere with me longer."

She had begun to speak with a recklessness and a savage irony that were shocking and repulsive; but in the end she spoke with a pathos and a passion that were irresistible. I was stirred to the bottom of my heart.

"I wish, dear lady," I said, "I wish you could know how deeply and sincerely I feel for you, how genuine and earnest my desire is to help you. Pray, pray give me at least a chance to do so. Look; I live in one of those houses, above there, on the terrace—where you see the lights. Come with me to my house. You say you have no roof under which you can seek a welcome: I will promise you a welcome there. You say you are friendless: let me be your friend. Come with me to my house. I believe—nay, I am sure—I shall be able in some way to help you. Anyhow, give me a chance to try. I am an old man, a physician. Come with me, and let us talk together. Between us we shall discover some better solution of your difficulties than the drastic one that you are looking to. But I will make a bargain with you. Come with me to my house, and remain there for one hour. If, at the expiration of that hour, I shall not have persuaded you to think better of your present purpose—if then you are still of your present mind—I will promise to let you depart unattended, without further hindrance, to go wherever and to do whatever you see fit. No harm can come to you from accompanying me to my house— no harm by any hazard, but possibly much good. Try it. Try me. Trust me.

Come. Within an hour, if you still wish it, you may go your way alone. I give you my word of honour. Will you come?"

"You leave me no free choice, sir. It will be my only means of deliverance from you. I run a great risk, a great peril, greater than you can think, in doing so. But it is agreed that at the end of one hour I shall be my own mistress again? After that—hands off?"

"At the end of one hour you may go or stay, according to your own pleasure."

"Very well; I am ready."

CHAPTER III.
WHENCE SHE CAME.

I led her into my back drawing-room—which apartment I use as a library and study—and turned up the drop-light on my writing-table.

Then I looked at her, and she looked at me.

She had said that she was young. I was not surprised to see that she was beautiful as well. I do not know that I can explain just what had prepared me for this discovery. Perhaps, in part, her voice, which was exquisitely sweet and melodious. Perhaps simply the tragical and romantic circumstances under which I had found her. However that may be, beautiful she indubitably was.

She wore no bonnet. Her hair, dark brown, curling, and abundant, was cut short like a boy's.

Her skin was fine in texture, and deathly pale. Her eyes, large, dark, liquid, were emotional and intelligent. Her mouth was generous in size, sensitive in form, and in colour perfect. But over her whole countenance was written legibly the signature of hard and fierce despair.

From throat to foot she was wrapped in a black waterproof cloak.

"Be seated," I began. "Put yourself at ease in mind and body. And first of all, let me offer you a glass of wine."

"You may spare yourself that trouble, sir," she replied. "I have no appetite for wine."

"But it will do you good. A single glass?"

"I will not drink a single drop."

"Well, then, a composing draught. You are my patient for the time being, remember. You must let me prescribe for you. You are in a state of excessive nervous excitement, bordering upon hysteria. Drink this."

"I assure you, sir, my disorder is not of the body," she said wearily. "No medicine can relieve it."

"Nevertheless, I will beg of you to give this a trial. It is but a thimbleful. It can't hurt you, even if it should fail to benefit you."

"For aught I know it may contain a drug."

"It certainly does contain a drug. I should not offer you *aqua pura*."

"You juggle words, sir. I mean a poison."

"Come; that is good. Do you think I would have been at such pains to dissuade you from suicide, immediately thereafter to seek to poison you?"

"I don't mean a deadly poison. You could do me no greater kindness than to offer me a deadly poison. I mean—it may contain some opiate, some narcotic, to deprive me of power over myself, so that I shall be unable to leave your house when the time is up."

"Madam, look at me. Have I the appearance of a man who would attempt to get the better of you by an underhand trick like that?"

"No, you do not look deceitful," she answered, after a moment's scrutiny of my face.

"Then trust me enough to drink this."

Without further protest she took the glass I proffered, and emptied it.

"Now, if you are willing, we may talk," said I.

"What is there to talk about? I, at any rate, have nothing to say. But I am at your mercy for the term of one hour. You, of course, may talk as much as you desire. But at the end of one hour—— Please look at your watch. What o'clock is it now?"

"It is twenty minutes after midnight."

"Thank you. Five minutes have already passed. At a quarter after one I shall be free to leave." Therewith she let her head fall back upon the cushion of the easy-chair in which she was seated, and closed her eyes.

"Yes," said I, "you will then be free to leave, if you still wish it. But I doubt if you will."

"Your doubt is groundless, sir. However, if it pleases you to cherish it, you may do so till the hour is finished."

"No, I cannot think my doubt is groundless. I told you I believed I should be able to show you a better way out of your troubles than the desperate one that you were purposing to take; and now I will make good my promise."

"Being more fully acquainted with my own affairs than you are, I assure you that your promise is one which cannot by any possibility be made good."

"Time will prove or disprove the truth of that assertion. To begin with, may I ask you a question or two?"

"You may ask me twenty questions. I do not pledge myself to answer them."

"Well, will you answer this one? Am I right in having understood you to say, when we were below there, on the wharf, that you have no friends or kindred whose feelings you are bound to consider in determining your conduct, and no worldly ties or associations which you are bound to respect?"

"Yes, you are right in that."

"I am right in having understood you to say that; but is what you said true?"

"Which would imply that you suspect me of having lied," she returned, with an unlovely smile. "Well, I don't blame you. I am a skilful and habitual liar, and I daresay it shows in my face. But in that case I broke my rule, and told the truth."

"My dear madam, I intended no such imputation. But you were agitated and excited; and sometimes under the stress of our excitement we unwittingly exaggerate."

"Well, I did not exaggerate. What I told you was literally true."

"And the rest that you said? That also you re-affirm? That you are penniless, homeless, wretchedly unhappy, and weary of life? It seems brutal for me to state it thus; but I must understand clearly, for a purpose which you will presently see."

"You need not apologise, sir. This is no occasion for mincing matters. Yes, I am penniless, homeless, wretchedly unhappy, and weary of life. But I am worse than that. I am bad. I am utterly base and degraded. Look at me," she added, fixing her eyes boldly, even defiantly, upon mine. "Examine me. I am a rare specimen. Very probably you have never seen my like before, and never will again. I am an example of—" she paused and laughed; and there was something in her laughter that made me shudder—"of total depravity," she concluded. Then suddenly her manner changed, and she became very grave. "Would you entertain a leper in your house, sir? Yet I have been told that I am a moral leper. I have been told that the corruption-spot upon me reaches in to the core. And I think my informant put it very moderately. If you suspected the crimes I have been guilty of, the worse crimes that I have meditated, and only failed to commit because of material obstacles that I could not overcome, you would not harbour me in your house for a single minute. You would feel that my presence was a contamination: that I polluted the chair I sit in, the floor under my feet. The glass I just drank from—you would shatter it into bits, that no innocent man or woman might ever put lips to it again. There! can't you see now that I am beyond help, beyond hope? What have I to live for? I am an incumbrance upon the face of the earth, and hateful to myself into the bargain. Why keep me here an hour? Let us rescind our compromise.* Let me go at once."

* It is possible that here and elsewhere Dr. Benary, in

reporting conversations from memory, puts into the mouths of *his interlocutors words and phrases from his own vocabulary,*

at the same time, without doubt, giving the substance and

the spirit of their remarks correctly. "Let us rescind our

compromise," at any rate, falling from the lips of a woman,

has, to say the least, an unrealistic sound.——-Editor.

She rose, and stood restive, as if expecting a dismissal.

"No, no; you must stay out your hour, at all events," I insisted. "Sit down again. I am sure you are not so black as you paint yourself; and in any case, guilt confessed and repented of is more than half atoned for."

"That is not so, to begin with," she retorted; "that is the shallowest, hollowest sort of cant. It may pass with people who know guilt only by hearsay, but is ridiculous to those who, like myself, have a knowledge of the subject at first hand.

"Guilt, crime, is atoned for only when it is undone, and all its consequences are obliterated. And now, speaking from my first-hand knowledge of the subject, I will tell you two things—first, all the confession and repentance in the world cannot undo a crime once done, nor obliterate its consequences; secondly, nothing can. You are a physician; I take it, therefore, you are familiar with the first principles of science: with what they call, I think, the Law of the Persistence of Force, the Law of the Conservation of Energy. If you understand that law, you will not dispute this simple application of it: a crime once done can never be undone; its consequences are ineradicable and eternal. Well and good. It is a puerility, in the face of the Law of the Persistence of Force, to talk of atonement. Atonement could come to pass only by means of a miracle—a suspension of Nature, and the interposition of a Supernatural Power. And that is where the Christians, with their dogma of vicarious atonement, are more rational than all the Rationalists from *a to zed*. So much for atonement. And now, as to repentance—who said that I repented? Repentance! Remorse! I will give you another piece of information, also speaking from firsthand knowledge. Repentance and Remorse are unmeaning sounds. There are no realities, no *things*, to correspond with them. I do not repent. No man or woman, from the beginning of time, has ever yet repented, in your sense of the word. We regret the losses that our crimes entail upon us: yes. We suffer because our crimes find us out, because retribution overtakes us: yes. But repent? We do not repent. Most of us pretend to. But I will be frank; I will not pretend.

"I suffer because the punishment which, by my crimes, I have brought down upon myself, is greater than I can bear; I suffer, too, because the last purpose

I had left to live for, which was also a criminal purpose, has been defeated. But I do not repent. I will not pretend to repent."

"Be all which as it may, I will repeat what I said before: I do not believe that you are so black as you paint yourself. You, young, beautiful, intelligent—no, no. But even if you were ten times blacker, it would make no difference to me. For, look you, since you have introduced a question of science, and favoured me with a scientific generalisation, I will pursue the question a little further, and cap your generalisation with another: namely, good, bad, or indifferent, we are not our own creators; we do not make ourselves; we are the resultants of our Heredity and our Environment; and our actions, whether criminal or the reverse, are determined not by free-will, but by necessity. I will not enlarge upon that generalisation; I will leave its corollaries for your own imagination to perceive. But in view of it, I will say again: even if you were ten times blacker, it would make no difference to me. You are no more to blame for the colour of your soul than for the colour of your hair."

"You are very magnanimous," she said bitterly, "and your doctrine would sound well in a criminal court."

"Think of me as scornfully as you will," I returned, "I am very sincerely anxious to befriend you."

"If that is true, you have it in your power to do so with marvellous ease."

"How so?" I queried.

"Absolve me from my agreement to stay here an hour. Sit still there in your chair, and let me go about my business unmolested and at once."

"No; to that agreement I must hold you, for your own sake. I have much to say to you, if you would only let me once get started."

"Good God, sir!" she cried, springing up in passion. "You drive me to extremes. Do you know that you are violating the laws of the State in harbouring me here?—that you are exposing yourself to the risk of prosecution?"

"I know that I should be violating the laws of humanity if I suffered you to lay violent hands upon yourself so long as I have it in my power to restrain you. As for the laws of the State, do you mean that you can bring an action against me for damages in interfering with your personal liberty? I doubt if you will do so. And I am sure no jury, apprised of the circumstances, would find against me."

"You are still in ignorance of the situation." said she. "Now open your eyes."

With that she threw off the waterproof cloak in which she was enveloped, and stood before me in the blue and white striped uniform of a Deadlock Island convict.

CHAPTER IV.
THE DOCTOR SPEAKS.

I confess my heart leapt into my throat, and I gasped for breath. She, witnessing my stupefaction, laughed, as if in cynical enjoyment of it.

After a little: "I think now you will permit me to bid you good evening," she said with mock ceremoniousness.

"You—you have escaped from prison!" I faltered out.

"Yes, from the Penitentiary across the river. You see, though we have never met until to-night, we have been neighbours, living within sight each of the other's residence, for some time. Two years already I have spent, somewhat monotonously, upon Deadlock Island; and, to employ technical language, I was 'in' for a term of which that was but an insignificant fraction. I had, however, certain business to transact here in town—a little matter to arrange with the gentleman who was the principal witness for the prosecution at my trial—and I seized, therefore, upon the first opportunity that presented itself to come hither incognito. But when I arrived I found that Fate, with her usual perversity, had put it out of my power to transact that business, the party of the second part having died from natural causes. Thus the one last only purpose I had left to live for had become impossible of accomplishment. And now I wish for nothing except death. At last even you must see the absurdity of my staying longer here in your house. Let me *go*."

"You say," I rejoined, having by this time recovered somewhat of my equanimity; "you say that you wish for nothing except death. Say what you will, I do not believe that you wish for death at all."

"To that I can only answer that you deceive yourself."

"No, it is you who deceive yourself. What you wish for is not death, but change—a change of condition. No truer words were ever spoken than those of Tennyson's:—

Whatever crazy sorrow saith,

No life that breathes with human breath

Has ever truly longed for death.

What you crave under the name of death is forgetfulness. You yourself compressed the whole truth into five words when you said: 'To live is to remember.' Your inference was that to die is to forget. It is memory that agonizes you; it is the past which lives in memory that handicaps you, that hangs like a mill-stone round your neck, and goads you to despair. If you could forget, if you could erase the entire past from your consciousness, you would cease to suffer. Is not that true?"

"True enough, perhaps. But without pertinence. A quibble. Forgetfulness is what I wish for, yes. But there is no forgetfulness except in death—no Lethe save the Styx."

"No forgetfulness *except* in death? You assume, then, that there *is* forgetfulness in death; a bold assumption. Have you no dread of something after death, the undiscovered country? Do you ignore the possibility of a future life? Suppose, beyond the grave, you preserve your identity—that is to say, your memory: in what respect will you have gained by the change?"

"I must take my risks. This much I know for certain: there is no forgetfulness in life. In death there may be. I will take my chances. Am I not in hell now? Any change must be a change for the better. I will take the risks."

"You say there is no forgetfulness in life. But suppose there were? Suppose it were possible for you to obtain total and permanent forgetfulness without dying, without taking those risks, without taking any risks at all? Suppose some one should come to you and say: 'See! I have it in my power to bestow upon you total and permanent obliviousness, so that the entire past, with all its events and circumstances, shall be perfectly effaced from your mind; so that you shall not even recall your name, nor your language; but, with unimpaired bodily health and mental capacities, shall begin life afresh, like the new-born infant, speechless, innocent, regenerated; another person, and yet the same:—suppose some one should come to you and offer that?"

"It is an idle supposition! The age of miracles has passed."

"An idle supposition? You deem it such? Let us see, let us consider. To begin with, answer me this: Have you never heard or read—in conversation, newspaper, medical report, or novel—have you never heard or read, I say, of a case where, through an accident, a human being has had befall him exactly the experience which I have just described? A case where a lesion of the cerebral tissues, caused perhaps by disease, perhaps by a concussion of the brain, or by a fracture of the skull, has resulted in the total annihilation of memory, without injury to the other intellectual faculties, so that the patient, upon recovering health and consciousness, could remember absolutely nothing of the past—neither his name, nor his nationality, nor the face of his father or mother, nor even how to speak, walk, eat—but was literally *born anew*, and had to begin life over again from the start? Surely, everybody who has ears has heard, everybody who can read has read, of cases of that nature?"

"Oh, yes; I have read of such cases, certainly."

"Very well. You have read of such cases. So!—Now, then, suppose an accident of that sort should befall *you?* Everything you can hope for from death would come to pass, and yet you would live. What better could you desire?

"And yet *I* would live? Hardly. My body would live, true. But *I*, my personality, my identity, would have vanished. For is not the very pith and marrow of one's identity, remembrance? Is not memory the birthmark, so to speak, by which one recognises one's-self? Is it not the cord upon which one's experiences are strung, which holds them together, and establishes their unity? My body would live, true enough. But it would be inhabited and animated by another spirit, another mind."

"Well, even so? It is the extinction of your identity which you seek to bring about by means of death. But you have no ground for supposing that death involves any such extinction. Atheist, agnostic, what you will, you must always acknowledge and allow for that possibility of a future life. Whereas, the man or woman to whom the accident happens which we have assumed, obtains for a surety that which he or she can only dubiously hope for from death."

"Ah, but there is a mighty difference. It is not within my power to cause such an accident. It *is* within my power to die."

"Not within your power to cause such an accident? Not within *your* power, I grant. But will you say that it is not within human power, not within any man's power? Imagine whatever human circumstance you like, which can come to pass by accident. Then, speaking *à priori*, tell me of any conclusive reason why that circumstance should not be brought to pass by design? Why man, investigating the causes of it, enlightened by his science, employing his cunning, should not be able at will to occasion it? Take this very case in hand—the total obliteration of a human being memory of the past. A blow upon the head, the result of an accident, can occasion it. Why not a blow upon the head, the result of man's deliberate purpose? Insanity, small-pox, consumption, paralysis, deafness, blindness—each of these it would be entirely possible for man voluntarily to induce. Why not oblivion?"

"I have never heard of its being done. I once read a novel in which something of the kind was related—'Dr. Heidenhoff's Process'—but even in that novel, the author had not the audacity to pretend that his story was possible; it turned out to be a dream. But then, after all, that was quite a different thing. It was the obliteration not of the whole memory, but simply the memory of one particular fact or group of facts. The memory in respect of other facts remained intact."

"Ah, that indeed! That, of course, it may not as yet be within the power of science to accomplish. That, as yet, I will grant you, is only the material for a romancer's fancy. I cannot cause you to forget any one fact or train of facts, while leaving your memory unaffected regarding other facts. But the obliteration of the whole memory is a very different matter. It has happened frequently by accident. You have never heard of its being effected by design, though you will acknowledge the theoretical possibility of its being so effected. Well and good. Now the truth is this: not only is it theoretically possible, but it is practically feasible.. It can be done; and I, even I, can do it. That same obliviousness which, as the case-books of physicians bear abundant testimony, Nature often produces through the medium of disease or violence, I—I who speak to you—I can produce by means of a surgical operation."

"It is incredible," said she.

"Incredible or not, it is a fact," said I. "What a stone striking you upon the head may accomplish, I can accomplish with my instruments. I can cause a depression of one of the bones of your skull, at a certain point upon the tissues of the brain, so that, when you recover from the influence of the anaesthetic which I administer, you are returned to the mental and moral condition of infancy. You remember nothing. You know nothing. Your mind is as a blank sheet of paper. The past is abolished. The future is before you."

"If what you say is true, you possess a terrible power. Are surgeons generally able to do this?"

"Every intelligent surgeon must recognise the antecedent possibility of the operation. But when you ask me whether surgeons generally know how to perform it, I suppose that they do not. It is a discovery which I have made, by the examination of a large number of skulls, and the dissection of a large number of brains. I have never communicated it to anybody else. Others, for all I know, may have made the same discovery independently."

"But why have you kept it a secret? It would have made you famous."

"I have had many reasons for keeping it a secret. You yourself have named one of them: it is a terrible power. I have not thought it prudent as yet to put it into the hands of the faculty at large; but it will be published after, if not before, my death."

"You say you *can* do this. *Have* you ever done it?"

"Upon a human being—no. Upon animals—upon dogs, monkeys, and horses—yes; often, and with unvarying success."

"Animals, indeed!" She smiled. "But never upon a human being. It is a descent from the sublime to the grotesque. You are anxious to obtain a subject?"

"I will not deny that I should be glad to obtain a subject, if it pleases you to put it in that downright way. I have never performed the operation upon a human being; but I can predict with absolute assurance just what its consequences upon a human being would be."

"Let me hear your prediction."

"Well, to begin with, let me tell you the circumstances of an actual case, which came under my observation, where the thing happened accidentally. The patient was a Frenchman, thirty-two years old, in robust health. I think, from the point of view of morals, he was the most depraved wretch it was ever my bad fortune to encounter. He was a brute, a sot, a liar, a thief—a bad lot all round. I chanced to know a good deal about him, because he was the husband of a servant in my family. The affair occurred more than thirty years ago. I say he was a depraved wretch. What does that mean? It means that, like every mother's son of us, he came into this world a bundle of potentialities, of latent spiritual potentialities, inherited from his million or more of ancestors, some of these potentialities being for good, others of them for evil; and it means that his environment had been such, and had so acted upon him, as to develop those that were for evil, and to leave dormant those that were for good. That wants to be borne in mind. Very well. He was the husband of a servant in my family, a most respectable and virtuous woman, also French, who would have nothing to do with him; but whom it was his pleasantest amusement to torment by hanging around our house, seeking to waylay her when she went abroad, striving to gain admittance when she was within doors. Late one evening we above stairs were surprised by the noise of a disturbance in the kitchen: a man's voice, a woman's voice, loud in altercation. I hurried down to learn the occasion of it. Halfway there, my ears were startled by the sudden short sound of a pistol-shot, followed by dead silence. I entered the kitchen, but arrived a moment too late. Our woman servant stood in the centre of the floor, holding a smoking revolver in her hand. Her husband lay prostrate, unconscious, perhaps dead, at her feet. I demanded an explanation. It appeared that he had stolen into the kitchen, where his wife sat alone, and, coming upon her suddenly, had attempted to abduct and carry her off by main force. The foolish woman confessed that some days before she had bought herself a pistol, with a view to just such an emergency as this; and now she had used it. Well, I examined the man, and I found, to my great relief, that he was not dead, and that, she being but an indifferent marks-woman, the ball had not even entered his body. It had struck him on the head at an oblique angle, and had glanced off. However, it had injured him quite seriously enough, having, indeed, fractured his skull at a certain point. We carried him upstairs, and put him to bed. For upwards of sixty hours—nearly three days—he lay in total unconsciousness. For six weeks he lay in a stupor just a hair's breadth removed from total unconsciousness; but by-and-by his wound had healed, and he was convalescent. Now, however, what was his mental condition? Precisely that of a new-born baby! His memory had been utterly destroyed. He had forgotten the simplest primary functions of life: how to speak, how to eat, how to walk, how to use his fingers. He could not remember his name; he could not recognise his wife. He had all the lessons of experience to learn anew. But you must recollect that, being an adult, his brain, as an organ, was full-grown, was mature. Therefore, he acquired knowledge with astonishing rapidity—learning almost as much in a fortnight as a child learns in a year. At the end of one month after we began his education, he could walk, feed himself, dress himself, and was beginning to talk. At the end of six months he spoke as fluently as I do—English, mind you, not French, which had been his mother-tongue. At the end of a year he read without difficulty, and wrote a good hand. What was most remarkable, however, though entirely natural, his moral nature had undergone a complete transformation. In a new environment, treated with kindness, surrounded by wholesome influences, 'trained up in the way he should go,' and absolutely oblivious of every fact, event, circumstance, and association of his past, he became a new, another, an entirely different man. Now, of the million spiritual potentialities, predispositions, that heredity had implanted in him, those that made for good were vivified, those that made for bad left dormant. He was as decent and as honest a fellow as one could wish to meet, and he had plenty of intelligence and common sense. I kept him in my service, as a sort of general factotum, for more than twenty years; then he died. Before his death he made a will, bequeathing to me the only thing of especial value that he had to leave behind him. Here it is."

I unlocked a cabinet, and produced from it a skull.

"Let me see it," she said eagerly.

She took it in her hands, without the faintest show of repugnance, and studied it intently.

"It is like a fairy-tale. It is marvellous," she said at last.

"Science abounds in marvels no less stupendous," said I. "It was my observation of that man's case, and of the beneficent results of it, that suggested to me the possibility of bringing such things to pass of a set, purpose."

"For years I have made the brain and the skull a study, with that possibility in view. I am able to say now that I can perform the operation with perfect certainty of success."

"But," she went on, after a pause, "it is scarcely inspiring to think that the character, the morality, of a human being, can be influenced, can be radically altered, by a mere physical condition like that—to think that the character of the soul can be changed by a change in the structure of the body. It is enough to establish materialism pure and simple; the only logical consequences of which are cynicism and pessimism."

"It is certainly one of the many psychological facts which go to prove that while it is the tenant of the body the soul must adapt itself to its habitation."

"It would seem to prove that the soul is not simply the tenant of the body, but its slave, its victim, its creature. As the materialists express it, that mind, thought, emotion, are but functions of the brain."

"It would perhaps lend colour to that hypothesis; but it does not prove it. Nothing can be proved relative to the human soul. Like all elemental things, it is in its very essence an insoluble mystery. All elemental things? Nay, it is *the* elemental thing, the ultimate thing, the only thing we know at first hand. All other things we know only as they are mirrored in it; we know them only by the impressions they produce upon our souls. Ten thousand hypotheses concerning it—concerning its origin, its nature, its meaning, its destiny—are equally plausible, equally inadequate. It cannot by seeking be found out."

She was silent now for a long while. At last, "Will you describe your operation to me?" she inquired.

"You would need a medical education to follow such a description."

"Is it anything like what they call trepanning, or trephining?"

"But very remotely. A partial fracture, and a depression, of the bone are caused; but no particle of it is removed."

"What is the worst that could happen, in case of the operation miscarrying? What would be the chances of the subject's losing not only his memory, but his reason—becoming an imbecile or a maniac?"

"There is no chance of that. The worst that could happen would be death. It is as safe an operation as any in which the knife is employed. But, of course, in all operations which involve the use of the knife there is some danger. There is always the possibility of inflammation. But that possibility is by no means a probability. The chances are largely against it."

"So that you are sure one of two things would happen either the operation would prove a success, or the patient would die?"

"Exactly so."

"How much time would have to elapse after the operation, before the patient would be able to take care of himself again—before he would have regained sufficient knowledge to act as a responsible and competent human being?"

"I should say a year. Perhaps more, perhaps less. But I will say a year."

"And during that year? Suppose, for example, that I should offer myself to you as a subject—how should I be provided for during the period of my incompetence? And what education should I receive?"

"You would be provided for by me. You would be lodged and taken care of here in this house. My sister, ten years younger than I, the kindest and the gentlest of women, would be your nurse, your companion, and your teacher. We would give you the same education that we would give a child of our own."

"I beg your pardon, but you have not told me your name."

"My name is Benary—Leonard Benary."

"Well, Dr. Benary, I am willing to submit to your operation. I make no professions of gratitude, for—though, whether it kills me or regenerates me, I shall be equally your debtor—I take it you are not sorry to find a subject to experiment upon; and therefore it will be a fair exchange, and no robbery. Will you proceed with the operation here, now, to-night?"

"Oh, dear me, no. You must have some sleep first. I will call my sister. She will show you to a room. Then, perhaps, to-morrow, after a good night's rest, you will be in a favourable condition."

"But your sister—what will she say to this?" She pointed to her prison-garb.

"If you will wait here while I go to summon her, I can promise you a kindly welcome from her. I shall explain all the circumstances to her; and she will not mind your costume."

And I went upstairs to rouse my sister, Miss Josephine Benary.

CHAPTER V.
THE DOCTOR ACTS.

Next morning, at about eleven o'clock, my good sister Josephine came to me in my study, and said, "She is awake now and wishes to see you."

"I am at her service," I replied. "Will she join me here?"

"She is eager to have you operate. She asked me where you would do so. I told her I supposed there, in her bed. Then she said she would not waste time by getting up, and wished me to tell you that she is waiting to have it done. I suspect that she is partly influenced by a reluctance to put on her prison uniform again. I should have offered her the use of my wardrobe, but she is so much taller and larger than I, that that would be absurd."

"Yes, to be sure, so it would. Very well. I will go to her directly. If she is in a favourable condition of mind and body, it will, perhaps, be as well not to delay. But first tell me—you have held some conversation with her?"

"Yes, a little."

"And what impression do you form of her character?"

"She is very pretty. She is even beautiful."

I laughed. "What has that to do with her character?99

"I infer her character as much from her appearance as from her behaviour, as much from her physiognomy as from her speech."

"Oh, I see. And your inference is?"

"I cannot be quite sure. There is a certain hardness in her face, a certain cynical listlessness in her manner, which may indicate a vice of character, but which may, on the other hand, result simply from hardship and suffering. She is undoubtedly clever. She has received a good education; she expresses herself well; she has a marvellously musical voice. Yet, on the whole, I cannot say that I find her likeable or agreeable. She seems to proceed upon the assumption that nobody is moved by any but selfish motives; that everybody has an axe to grind; and that she must be constantly on her guard lest we take some advantage of her. She is horribly suspicious."

"Well, go on."

"Well, I do not know that I can say anything more. I cannot quite fathom her—quite make her out. It is a question in my mind whether she is naturally a young woman of good instincts, whose passions have betrayed her into the commission of some crime, or whether she is inherently and intrinsically corrupt."

"Towards which alternative do you incline?"

"I do not like to express a final opinion; but I am afraid, from what little I have seen of her, I am afraid that I incline towards the latter."

"That she is intrinsically bad. Well, it will be interesting, after our operation, to see whether, in a new environment, under new conditions, the good that is latent in her—as good is latent in every human soul—will be developed. And now will you come with me to her room?"

"Will she not prefer to see you alone?"

"Why should she? Come, let us go."

We found her sitting up in bed, waiting for us. By daylight she seemed to me even more beautiful than she had seemed by gaslight. Her features were strongly yet finely modelled; her skin was exquisitely delicate, both in texture and in colour; and her eyes were wonderfully liquid and translucent. But an expression of deep melancholy brooded over her whole countenance; while underlying that again, was certainly visible the cynical hardness that Josephine had complained of.

Having wished her good-morning, I proceeded at once to my business as a physician; ascertained her pulse and her temperature, and inquired how she had slept.

"I have not had such a night's sleep for I know not how long," she answered. "Heaven knows I had enough to think about to keep me awake, yet I must have lain in total unconsciousness for fully nine hours. What was most grateful, I did not dream. All which leads me to suspect that, despite your protestations to the contrary, the medicine you made me drink last evening contained an opiate."

"The medicine I prevailed upon you to drink last evening," I explained, "was the mildest composing-draught known to the Pharmacopoeia—a most harmless mixture of orange-flower water, bromide, and sugar. If it had the effect of a sleeping-potion, I am very glad to learn it, for it indicates the degree of your nervous susceptibility—a point upon which it is highly desirable that I should be informed. And are you still of the same mind in which I left you? You have not reconsidered your determination?"

"No. I am still ready to be killed or regenerated—I am really quite indifferent which. When I awoke this morning, I could not help fancying that the conversation which I seemed to recall had never really taken place—that I had dreamed it. But this lady, your sister, assures me that my doubt is groundless. Now I can only request you to begin and get over with it as soon as possible."

"My beginning must be in the nature of an interrogatory. I must ask you for certain information."

"Very well. Ask."

"My questions shall be few: only those formal ones which, as a physician, I should put to any patient whom I was about to treat. First, then, what is your name?"

"My name is Louise Massarte, spelt M-a-s-s-a-r-t-e."

I opened my case-book, prepared my fountain-pen for action, and wrote "Louise Massarte."

"It is a foreign name, is it not?" I inquired "Were you born in this country?"

"Like the other hopeful subject of whom you told me last night, I was born in France—at the city of Tours."

"Native of France," I wrote. Then aloud s "Of French parents?"

"Yes, I am French by descent and by place of birth. But I have lived in America all my life. I was brought here when I was two years old."

"But you speak French, I take it?"

"I speak French and English with equal ease."

"Any other language?"

"No other."

"How old are you, if you will forgive my asking?"

"I shall be six-and-twenty on the eighth of August."

"Are your parents living?"

"Both my father and mother are long since dead."

"Have you any brothers or sisters?"

"I was an only child."

"Are you married or single?"

"I have never been married."

"And now, finally, is there any fact or circumstance which you would like to mention and have recorded? For, you must bear in mind, you will shortly have forgotten everything connected with your past; and if there is anything you will wish to remember, you had better tell it to me now, and I will make a memorandum of it."

"There is nothing that I shall wish to remember," she replied. "Nothing but what I shall be glad to forget. However, I fancy what you say is but a hint to the effect that you are curious to know my history. I have no objection in telling it to you. It is not an edifying history. Most women, I daresay, would be ashamed to tell it; but I have got beyond even pretending to feel ashamed of anything; and if you desire to hear it, you have only to say so."

"On the contrary," I rejoined, "you must not think of telling it. It would excite you and fatigue you; whereas it is of the highest importance for the success of our operation that you should be at rest in mind as well as in body. Besides, and irrespective of that consideration, it is better that neither my sister, nor I, nor indeed any living person, should hear it. You yourself will in a little while have forgotten it. What right has anybody else to remember it?"

"Oh, well, you will doubtless find the gist of it in the morning paper. It will in all likelihood be printed with an account of my escape from the Penitentiary," she returned.

At which insinuation my sister Josephine cried out, "You little know my brother. There is indeed something about your escape in the morning paper; but the instant he discovered the headlines of the article, he said, 'This is something, Josephine, that neither you nor I must read.' And he threw the paper into the fireplace, and applied a match to it."

The woman made no answer.

I left the room and descended to my study, where I procured my instruments and the requisite anæsthetic.

CHAPTER VI.
MIRIAM BENARY.

I watched her carefully as she recovered from the effects of the ether. An uncommonly small quantity of that drug had sufficed to deprive her of her senses; and now her recovery was unusually speedy.

Having taken her respiration, her temperature, and her pulse, and having found each to be nearly normal, I looked her straight in the eyes, and demanded, making every syllable clear and emphatic, "Louise Massarte, do you know me?"

Had I addressed my inquiry to a month-old infant, the result would have been the same.

I repeated the question in French: "Louise Massarte, *me reconnaissez vous?*"— with precisely the same negative result.

I then wrote the question both in French and English upon a slip of paper, and held it before her eyes.

No sign of intelligence.

In the end I applied tests to each of her five senses, and satisfied myself that each was unimpaired.

After which, "Well, Josephine," I said, "unless all signs fail, we have succeeded to admiration. None of her senses have sustained the slightest injury, yet she has lost the knowledge of language, both spoken and written. Louise Massarte is dead, annihilated, abolished from the face of creation. This is a new-born infant, this apparently full-grown woman lying here. Her soul is still to develop and unfold itself. It will be for us to shape it, to colour it, to direct it towards good or evil. Heredity has furnished the capacities, the propensities, which her environment will quicken, stimulate, cause to grow and to ripen. And it is for us to provide and to regulate that environment. May Heaven guide our labours."

"Amen, heartily. It is an awful responsibility. And yet————"

"And yet?"

"And yet I cannot help hoping for the best. Look at her, brother. See how beautiful she is. Surely, such a beautiful face must be meant to go with a beautiful spirit. Already the expression of bitterness, of hardness, of suspicion, seems to have faded from it. It is as if it had been washed in some element infinitely cleansing. I never saw a more innocent face than hers has become already. Yes, I am sure we may hope for the best."

"Well, for the present, we need concern ourselves only for the welfare of her body. We must darken the room. Inflammation is the only ill consequence we have to fear; and that can be averted, if we keep her in darkness and in silence until the wound has healed."

The wound healed quickly. Not an unpleasant symptom of any kind manifested itself. And, as I had foreseen she would do, our patient relearned the primary lessons of life with an ease and a rapidity that seemed almost incredible. I had anticipated this because she was an adult; because, that is to say, her brain, as an organ, was of mature development.

She began to speak as soon as ever we allowed ourselves to speak in her presence, at first simply imitating the sounds we made, but very speedily coming to employ words with understanding. A single lesson taught her how to walk. After my sister had dressed her twice, she was perfectly well able to dress herself—no trivial achievement when the intricacy of the feminine toilet is borne in mind. At the end of an incredibly short period of time she could read and write as easily as I can. Of the former capability she made good use, devouring eagerly all such books as we thought wise to give her. Her progress, in a word, precisely corresponded to that made by a bright child, only it was infinitely more rapid; and what a fascinating thing it was to observe, I need not stop to tell. It was like watching the growth and blossoming of some most wonderful and beautiful flower. We were permitted, so to speak, to be eye-witnesses of a miracle. If you had met her at the expiration of one year, and had conversed with her, you would have put her down for a singularly intelligent and well-informed, yet at the same time singularly innocent and unsophisticated, girl of eighteen. Yes, I mean it—a girl of eighteen. For the most astonishing result of my operation—most astonishing because least expected—was this: that in body as well as in mind she seemed to have been rejuvenated. With the obliteration of her memory, every trace of experience faded from her face. You would have laid a wager that it was the face of a young maiden not yet out of her teens. She had said that she was all but six-and-twenty. It was unbelievable when you looked at her now. To the desperate-eyed woman whom I had dissuaded from self-destruction on that clouded Bummer's night a year gone by, she bore only such a resemblance as a younger sister might have borne. To Josephine I remarked, "Is it possible that we have builded better than we knew? That we have stumbled upon the discovery which the alchemists sought in vain—the Elixir of Youth?"

"Indeed," Josephine assented, "she has grown many years younger. She has the appearance and the manner of seventeen."

"It only proves," said I, "the truth of the oft-repeated commonplace: that it is experience and not time which ages one; time being simply the receptacle and measure of experience. Could we double the rate of our experience—experiencing as much in one year as we are now able to experience in two—we should grow old just twice as quickly, reaching at thirty-five the limit which we now reach at threescore-and-ten. Contrariwise, could we halve the rate of our experience—requiring two years to experience what we can now experience in one—we should grow old just twice as slowly, being mere boys at forty, and at seventy in the very prime of early manhood. Our consciousness of time, in other words, is simply the consciousness of so much experience. Well and good. Now, in this case, her experience has been undone. That is to say, her memory, the storehouse of her experience, has been destroyed. Past time, so far as it affects her mind, has been neutralised, has been cancelled out of her equation. Hence this return to adolescence. Her bodily structure—the size and shape of her bones, and all that—of course remains as it was. But her spirit returns to the condition of youth; and, since it is the spirit which animates the body, it gives to her body the expression and the activity of its own age."

Then I offered to perform my operation upon Josephine herself, to the end that she also might enjoy a restored youth: which offer Josephine haughtily declined.

"It is very fortunate," she added, "that this alteration in her appearance has taken place, for now it will be impossible for anybody who may have known her in former days to identify her: a danger which otherwise we should have had to fear."

"Yes," I acquiesced, "that is very true."

The disposition which our visitor developed, furthermore, better than answered to our most sanguine anticipations. Her new environment vivified the best of those propensities which heredity had implanted in her, and left dormant those that were for evil. Her quality was so sweet and winning, that in a little while she had taken our old hearts captive, and become the delight and the treasure of our home. We loved her like a daughter; and the notion that we might some time have to part with her was intolerable. Therefore, we put our heads together, and entered into a pious conspiracy, agreeing to represent to her that she was our niece, the child of our brother, an orphan, eighteen years old, by name Miriam, who, on the 14th day of June, 1884, had sustained an accident which had destroyed her recollection of the past. As our niece, recently arrived from England, we introduced her to our friends. She reciprocated our affection in the tenderest manner, called us aunt and uncle, and was in every respect a blessing to our lives—so beautiful, so gentle, so merry, so devoted.

This mysterious and impressive circumstance I must not for one moment allow to be lost sight of:—That, of all living human beings, she who least suspected that such a woman as Louise Massarte had ever lived, sinned, suffered, was Miriam Benary. She upon whom Louise Massarte's life, sins, and sufferings had least effect or influence, was Miriam Benary. Her identity was in every respect as separate, and as distinct from that of Louise Massarte, as mine is from my reader's. Louise Massarte was dead, dead utterly. Into her tenement of clay a new soul had entered It was a fearful and wonderful metamorphosis, rich in suggestiveness; a *datum*, it seems to me, bearing importantly upon three sciences: Psychology, Divinity, and Ethics.

Thus nearly four years elapsed, and it was Monday, the 12th day of March, 1888, the day of the memorable snowstorm, called the Blizzard.

CHAPTER VII.
WITHIN AN ACE.

On that day certain imperative business demanded my presence in the lawyer's quarter of the town. I had been summoned, in short, to appear as a witness in a litigation that was pending in the Court of Common Pleas—a summons which I felt myself the more disposed to obey inasmuch as a penalty of two hundred and fifty dollars attached to contempt of it. Therefore, despite the unprecedented brutality of the weather, and against the earnest remonstrances of Josephine and Miriam, I was foolhardy enough to venture out.

The clock on our drawing-room mantel marked a few minutes before ten when I left the house, my immediate destination being the Jefferson Street Station of the Overhead Railway—distant not more than a quarter of a mile from my own door, and in ordinary circumstances an easy five minutes' walk.

However, it must be remembered, I was at that time within a few months of completing my seventieth year; and such a storm was raging, and such a gale blowing, as might have strained the mettle of a youngster one third my age: a veritable tempest, indeed, the like of which Adironda had never in the memory of man experienced before. The mercury stood below zero Fahrenheit; the wind was travelling at the pace of sixty miles an hour; and the snow was falling in such unheard of quantities as to obscure the air like fog. I don't mind owning, therefore, that I was pretty badly exhausted when I arrived at my journey's end, and that I had consumed a good half-hour in the process of getting there.

My path, as it were, had led through one continuous and unbroken drift, knee-deep at its shallowest, waist-high at its average, and frequently engulphing me up to my chin. Through this I had dug and ploughed my way, with the wind cold and furious in my teeth, and under a running fire of snow-flakes, frozen so hard, and driven with such force, that they stung my face like bird-shot, and nearly put out my eyes. I can assure the reader that it was no child's play. My nose and ears, from burning as if in a bath of scalding water, had become numb and rigid, like features of wood. The moisture from my breath had congealed in my beard, until that appendage felt like an iron mask. My legs were stiff and heavy. My shoulders ached. My respiration had become painful and laborious; my heart-action so faint as to induce sickness similar to that which one suffers at sea.

And finally, to cap the climax, when I reached the station, I found a chain stretched across the entrance to the booking-office, and a placard announcing that no trains were running! So that I had earned my labour for my pains; and there was nothing for me to do but to turn my face back toward home, and retrace my steps.

Exhausted as I was, then, I set forth at once upon that undertaking. Of course, it was excessively imprudent for me to do so, without first seeking shelter in some public house, and resting there until I had got warmed through, and in a measure recovered my strength. But I suppose I did not realise at the moment how far gone I was; and the prospect of regaining the comfort of my own fireside was a deliciously tempting one. So off I started, down Jefferson Street, towards Myrtle Avenue.

Very soon, however, I had reason to repent my rashness. A hundred yards or thereabouts from the corner, a mountainous drift of snow stretched diagonally across the road. I was half blinded; my wits were half frozen; I underestimated both its depth and its width, and plunged boldly into it.

Next instant I found myself buried up to my neck.

I struggled to push on. My legs were as immovable as if bound with ropes.

Then I strove to dig myself free with my hands. My arms, too, I learned, were pinioned as in a strait-waistcoat.

Here was a pleasant predicament, and one that constantly increased in interest; for, to say nothing of the deadly and aggressive cold, the snow was pouring down upon me by the bucket-full; and I appreciated very vividly the fact that unless I speedily effected an escape, I should be covered over my head.

My only hope, it was obvious, lay in calling for assistance. Whether other human beings were within hearing distance or not, I had no means of discovering; for, so opaque was the atmosphere rendered by the multitude of snow-flakes that filled it, I could see nothing beyond a radius of two or three yards; and even the houses that lined the street were indistinguishable, except when, by fits and starts, for a second at a time, the wind rent asunder the veil that hid them. Nevertheless, my only hope lay in trying the experiment of a cry for help; and that accordingly I did, with the utmost energy I could command:

"Help! help!"

But at the sound of my voice, my heart sank. It was the still, small ghost of itself, to such a degree had the exposure and the hardship of the last half-hour depleted my physical resources; and besides, dampened by the blanket of snow in which I was enveloped, and lost in the roar of the hurricane, the likelihood that it would carry beyond a rod in any direction seemed infinitesimally slight.

"Well, I am lost," thought I. "Here, not five hundred yards from my own doorstep, lost as hopelessly as if wrecked in mid-ocean. Ah, well! they say death by freezing is comparatively painless. Anyhow, it will soon be over. Yet——"

Suddenly, with the desperate unreasonableness of a man in extremities—like him who, drowning, clutches at a chip—I repeated my feeble signal of distress: "Help! help!"

I waited half a minute, and then repeated it for a third time: "Help!"

Conceive my emotions, to hear instantly, and from immediately behind me, the response, in the lustiest of baritones: "Hello, there!"

"Heaven be praised!" I gasped. Then: "Can you help me out of this drift?"

"That remains to be tried," came the reply. "I shouldn't wonder, though."

And therewith I felt myself seized by two strong arms, lifted bodily from off my feet, and a moment later set down upon a spot of the pavement which the wind had swept clean, where I had a chance to see and to thank my rescuer.

CHAPTER VIII.
A CHANCE ACQUAINTANCE.

He was a tall and athletic-looking man, perhaps thirty years old, with a ruddy, good-humoured face, an honest pair of blue eyes, and a curling yellow beard. He wore a sealskin cap which came down over his ears, sealskin gloves which reached up above his coat-sleeves nearly to his elbows, a pea-jacket, and rubber top-boots. His beard, his eyebrows, and so much of his hair as was exposed, were dense with frozen snow, and from his moustache depended a series of icicles, like tusks, where his breath had condensed and congealed.

"I believe I have to thank you for saving my life," I began, in such voice as I could muster, and I noticed that my utterance was thick, like that of a drunken man. "A very little more and I had been done for."

"Yes, you were in rather a nasty box," he admitted. "But all's well that ends well; and you're safe enough now. When I heard you calling, I thought it was a child, your voice was so thin and faint."

"It's highly fortunate for me that you heard me at all. I had given myself up for lost. What a storm this is!"

"Yes; glorious, isn't it? It's the grandest spectacle I've ever seen. I tell you, sir, it's well for us that Nature should occasionally show us her sharp claw; otherwise we'd get to considering her a quite tame domestic pet, which she's not by any means. She's man's hereditary foe; there stands a perpetual feud between her and us, a *vendetta* handed down from father to son, from generation to generation. It's only by the exercise of an eternal vigilance and industry that we manage to subsist in spite of her. She's constantly striving, one way or another, to exterminate us: freeze us out, roast us out, starve us out—I know not what all. Here we are, huddled together upon this bleak, mysterious planet, parasites upon its surface, like mould on cheese, sheltering ourselves in fortresses of straw—wondering whence we came, why we're here, whither we're bound, and what the fun of the whole thing is—while she whirls us through her dark immensities, and seeks hourly to shake us off; which is rather unmannerly of her, seeing it was she herself who brought us here. Life which she gives us with one hand, she withholds with the other. She begrudges what she lavishes. Oh, it is strange, it is magnificent; it's some grand paradoxical farce, which we haven't wit enough to see the point of. Still, there's an exhilaration in the conflict, unequal though it is. She's sure to win in the end; she plays with us like a cat with a mouse, amused at our desperate antics, but confident of her power to administer a quietus when they begin to pall; yet there's a pleasure, somehow, in the struggle. They say, you know, the fox enjoys being hunted. To-day she's in a particularly frolicsome mood, and puts vim into her buffets. For my part, I'm grateful to her. She'll laugh best, because she'll laugh last; but she can't prevent my relishing my laugh meanwhile. I have not lived in vain, who have lived to experience this storm. Isn't it stimulating? I vow, it makes a man feel like a boy."

I had stood shivering, teeth chattering, while he delivered himself of this extraordinary harangue. Now, "That would depend somewhat upon the age and the physique of the man," I stammered.

"Why, yes, true enough. Your observation is altogether apposite and just. But for me, I declare, it is like wine. Which way do you go?"

"I go east and south—to my home, which is in Riverview Road, if you know where that is. But to tell you the truth, I doubt my ability to go at all. *I'm* pretty badly used up. I think I shall ask to be taken in at one of these neighbouring houses."

"As you like it. But I know where River-view Road is; in fact I'm bound in that direction myself, being curious to see how the storm affects the Yellow Snake. It must be a sight for the gods—the writhing and the lashing of the reptile river under such a wind. If you please we'll march together. I suspect, with my assistance, you'll be able to arrive."

"You've already saved my life, and now you offer to see me safely home. I shall owe you a heavy debt. But I could never consent to take you out of your way."

"As I've already had the honour to intimate, that's precisely what you won't do. I was bound for the riverside—upon my word. Come on."

And the next thing I knew, my robust interlocutor had again lifted me from my feet, and was trudging off towards Myrtle Avenue, bearing me like a child in his arms—which, of course, was altogether too ignominious a position for me to occupy without protest.

"Oh, this is needless. I beg of you to put me down. Really, I can't submit to this. Let me walk at your side, and lean upon your arm, and I shall do very well."

"My dear sir," he rejoined, "permit me to observe—and I beseech you not to resent the observation as personal—that if ever a mortal man was completely tuckered out, you are. You've lost your wind, and your legs are as shaky as if you had the palsy. Pardon my austere frankness—the circumstances compel it. You couldn't get as far as the corner yonder to save your neck. You are, to employ the politest of modern languages, *hors de combat*. You are *ansgespielt*, you are *non compos corporis*—that is to say, in pure Americanese, you are *busted*. Now, so far as I am concerned, on the contrary, I don't mind carrying you any more than I would a baby. At the outside you don't weigh ten stone; and what's the like of that to a fellow of my horse-power? Lie still, and I sha'n't know you're there. Lie still and rest, recover your breath, and be yourself again."

"But the thing is too ridiculous. I can't in dignity consent to it, I entreat you to put me down."

I attempted to release myself, but his arms were like bands of iron.

"There, there—resign yourself! I prithee, wriggle not," he said. "I shall put you down presently—when the time is ripe. And as for your dignity, remember the device of Cæsar: *Esée quant videri*. This, sir, is an occasion for choosing between appearances and a very grim reality. I can understand that, other things equal, you wouldn't care to have the world see us in our present situation; but console yourself with the reflection that the storm answers every purpose of a dose of fern-seed, and renders us beautifully invisible. Anyhow, I take it, your dignity isn't as precious to you as your health; and I will go bail for this, that if you tried to foot it another hundred yards, you'd pay for your temerity with a fit of sickness. Consider, furthermore, that I am old enough to be your son. Let me play a son's part for the nonce, and carry you home."

"Well, I have no right to quarrel with you," I answered; "but you place me under an obligation which I shall never be able to discharge. It will bear as heavily upon my conscience as I now weigh upon your muscles."

"Then it will cause you mighty slight annoyance. To tell you the truth, it's a jolly good lark for me. It's an added excitement, a most interesting adventure; and it will provide a capital chapter for the winter's tale that I shall have to tell. But a truce to talk. Let's waste no further breath in that way. You lie still there and meditate. I'll devote my energies to the business of getting on."

So for a good while we forbore speech. At length, "Now, then," he announced, "here's Riverview Road. Our toilsome journey's o'er; and, all our perils past, in harbour safe at last we rest. What would you more?—What's your number?"

"Sixty-three, the fourth house from the corner."

"Well, here you are on your own doorstep.—There!"

He set me upon my feet.

"And now, sir," he concluded, "trusting that you may suffer no ill effects from your experience, I will wish you farewell. Farewell, a long farewell. This is a life made up of partings. Again, farewell."

"Farewell by no manner of means," I hastily retorted. "You must come in. You must do me the honour of entering my house, and allowing me to offer you some refreshment. And besides, if, as you said, you are anxious to watch the play of the storm upon the river, you could possess no better coigne of vantage than one of my back windows."

"Such an inducement, sir, is superfluous. Your invitation in itself would be quite irresistible. For, aside from the pleasure I derive from your society, and the instruction from your conversation, I will confidentially admit to you that I shall be glad to thaw out my nose."

I opened the door with my latch-key, and preceded him into my study.

***

CHAPTER IX.
JOSEPHINE WRITES.

A beautiful fire was blazing in the grate. The transition from the cold and uproar of the street, to the snug quiet and warmth of this cosy book-lined room, was an agreeable one, I can tell you. I was pretty well rested by this time; and, except for the tingling of my nose, ears, toes, and fingers, felt very little the worse for my encounter with the elements.

"Now," said I to my guest, "the tables are turned. But a moment since, I was your prisoner; now you are mine. Draw up to the fire. Throw off your over jacket and your rubber-boots. I hope you are not wet through; for, we are built respectively upon such different patterns, it would be ironical for me to offer you dry garments from my wardrobe."

"You need give yourself no uneasiness upon that score, sir. Im as dry as a Greek lexicon."

"In that case, let me at once offer you a drop of something wet," I said, producing a decanter and a couple of glasses.

"Yes," he assented, "a toothful of this will do neither of us harm."

We clinked our glasses, and drank.

"Ah," he cried, smacking his lips, "sweet ardent spirit of the rye, may the shade of Christopher Columbus be fed upon you thrice every day, to reward him for the discovery of this continent. I've tasted Irish and I've tasted Scotch, Dutch barley-brandy and Slavonic vodka; but of all distillations to make glad the inmost heart of man, give me Kentucky rye! Another glass? Thank you, kind sir, not e'en another drop. 'Twere desecration worthy only of a widower to take a second after so rare a first. And now, by-the-bye, since I find myself the beneficiary of your hospitality, it behoves me to introduce myself. My name is Henry Fairchild, and by trade I am a sculptor."

"My name is Leonard Benary, physician and surgeon. And I trust, Mr. Fairchild, that you have no urgent affairs to call you from my house, for I should never feel easy in my mind if I permitted you to leave it before this storm has abated; and that doesn't look like an imminent event. My affairs are not urgent. In fact, as I believe I have already remarked, when we ran across each other I was abroad for my diversion, pure and simple. But that is no reason why I should abuse your kindness. If I may thaw here before your fire for a half-hour, I shall be in perfect condition to make my way home."

"That would depend upon the distance of your home from mine."

"My home is in my studio. And my studio is in St. Matthew's Park."

"So far! Very well, then. I shall certainly not hear of your leaving me so long as the storm continues. It would be as much as your life is worth to attempt such a journey in such circumstances. It's a matter of three, four, well-nigh five miles. And since all public conveyances are at a standstill, you'd have to trust yourself for the whole distance to Shanks's mare. I shall count upon your spending the night here, at least. There's no prospect of the weather moderating before to-morrow. And now, if you will excuse me, I will leave you here for a few moments, while I go to change my clothes."

"That's the wisest thing you could possibly do," he returned. "I shall amuse myself excellently looking out of the window; but as for your kind invitation to remain over night——"

"As for that, since you acknowledge that you have no pressing business to call you elsewhere, I will listen to no refusal."

I went upstairs, my first care being to make known my return to Josephine and Miriam, who, of course, were thereby greatly surprised and relieved. They professed they had suffered the acutest anxiety ever since I had left the house; and as they listened to the account I gave them of my misadventures, they paled and shuddered for very terror.

"Mr. Fairchild, the young man who came to my rescue, is even now below stairs in the library," I concluded.

"Oh, is he? Then," cried Miriam, addressing Josephine, "let us go to him at once, and tell him how we thank him. To think that, except for him, my uncle might——" She completed her sentence by putting her arms around my neck, and giving me three of the sweetest kisses that were ever given in this world: one on either cheek and one full on the lips. "Now, sir," she went on, shaking the prettiest of fingers at me, "I hope that you have learned a lesson, and will never do anything again that we two wise women warn you not to."

"I promise to be a good, obedient, little old man in the future," I replied; and was rewarded for my docility with a fourth kiss—this time imprinted among the wrinkles on my forehead.

The two wise women went off downstairs.

I joined them as soon as I had got into dry clothing; and we sat down to luncheon—the young sculptor enlivening and entertaining us with a flow of droll, high-spirited talk. He and Miriam got on famously together—chatting, laughing, exchanging bits of repartee, with the vivacity that was becoming to their age. Josephine and I hearkened and enjoyed. At least, I enjoyed; and I had no reason to suppose that my sister did not. Luncheon concluded, we adjourned to the drawing-room. There, observing the piano, Fairchild demanded of Miriam whether she played. She answered, "Yes." (We had procured for her the best musical instruction to be had in Adironda; and she had mastered the instrument with a facility which proved that Louise Massarte must have been a talented pianist.) Miriam answered, "Yes," and then Fairchild said—

"Will you not be persuaded to play for us now?"

She played one of Liszt's Hungarian Rhapsodies, and then something of Chopin's, and then something of Schumann's; after which, leaving the piano, she said to Fairchild—

"Now you must sing for us."

"Why, how do you know I can sing?" cried he.

"It is evident from the *timbre* of your voice," she answered.

"You must not be too sure of that," he protested. "The speaking voice and the singing voice are two very different things."

"Nevertheless, please sing for us," she repeated.

"Very good," said he, taking possession of the key-board, "I will sing for you; but at your peril. The beauty of the song, however, may perhaps be allowed to atone for the deficiencies of my execution. It is by the English composer, Marzials, a man of the rarest genius, too little known out of his own country. He wrote both words and music, and the song is entitled 'Never Laugh at Love.'"

Therewith, to his own accompaniment, he sang in his sweet baritone one of the pleasantest and wittiest songs of its kind that I have ever heard.

Oh, never laugh at Love, Miss, fancy free,

Lest the wanton boy should laugh at thee!

Should he but aim in play his tiny dart—

Ping! 't will break your heart!

I knew a queen with golden hair,

Few so proud, and none so fair;

Her maids and she, one twilight gray,

Went wand'ring down the garden way.

A pretty page was standing there;

Their eyes just met. Oh, long despair!

For both have died of love, they say.

So never laugh at Love, Miss, fancy free,

Lest the wanton boy should laugh at thee!

I cannot forbear quoting that one verse, to give a notion of the quaint mediæval charm of the words. * I wish I could transcribe the melody as well, which was delicious with the same quaint flavour.

    The Editor of this work must disclaim all responsibility

    Dr. Benary's opinions upon matters literary and aesthetic.

Fairchild having finished his song, he and Miriam plunged into an animated conversation about music in the abstract, which I, for one—being, though an ardent lover of music, no musician—found of dubious interest.

"Wherefore, I think," I interrupted them to say, "if you will forgive the breach of ceremony, Mr. Fairchild, I shall retire to my bedroom for a bit, and take a nap. I feel somewhat fatigued after the exertions of the forenoon; and, anyhow, I am accustomed to my forty winks at this hour of the day. I am sure I leave you in good hands when I leave you to my sister and my niece."

"Indeed, Dr. Benary, the kindest thing you can do for me—you and your good ladies—will be to let me feel that in no wise do I interfere with your convenience or your pleasure. Otherwise, I shall be compelled to take my departure *instanter*; and I confess that by this time I am so deeply penetrated by the comfort of your interior that I should hate mortally to renew close quarters with the storm."

So I withdrew to my bed-chamber, and was sound asleep in no time. Nor did I wake till the mellow booming of the Japanese gong, which serves as dinner-bell in our establishment, broke in upon my slumbers.

As I rose to my feet, something dropped from the counterpane to the floor.

Stooping to pick it up, I discovered that it was a sheet of paper, folded in the form of a cocked hat, and bearing my name written across it in Josephine's hand.

"What earthly occasion can Josephine have for writing me a note?" I wondered.

Donning my spectacles, I read as follows:

"What ever shall we do? I cannot come and say this to you in person, for I dare not leave them alone together. But he has recognised Miriam!—J."

It took fully a minute for the significance of that sentence: "He has recognised Miriam," to percolate my understanding, still thick with the dregs of sleep. Then I started as if I had been stung; and rushing into the passage, I called "Josephine! Josephine!" at the top of my lungs.

CHAPTER X.
JOSEPHINE EXPLAINS.

The passage was quite dark. From the end of it, directly behind me, came the response, "Yes, Leonard."

"Ah, you are there?" I questioned.

"I have been waiting for you to wake. I did not wish to disturb your sleep," she explained.

"And they—where are they now?"

"Mr. Fairchild is in the guest-chamber, where he is to sleep. Miriam is in her room. I could not come to you so long as they were together. It would not do to leave them alone. That is why I wrote the note."

By this time we were between my own four walls, and I had closed the door behind us.

"And now, for Heaven's sake, explain to me what this means," I said, holding up the sheet of paper.

"It means what it says. He has recognised Miriam."

"Oh, it is impossible," I declared.

"I only wish you were right," sighed Josephine dolefully.

"But how—but why—but what—what makes you think so?" stammered I.

"His action when he first saw her—when she and t entered the room where he was, to greet him, this forenoon."

"Oh, it is impossible—impossible!" I repeated, helplessly. "What was his action? What did he do?"

"He caught his breath, he started, he coloured up, and then turned white, and then red again."

"Merciful Heavens!" I gasped, panic-stricken.

"What shall we do? What can we do?" my poor sister groaned.

"Did—did Miriam notice his embarrassment?"

"I think not. She did not appear to, anyhow."

There befell a pause, during which I tried to collect my wits, and to reflect upon the situation.

"Well," persisted Josephine, after the silence had continued for a minute or two, "what shall we do?"

"It is impossible, it is absolutely impossible," I said. "Her own mother would be unable to recognise her. She is altered beyond recognition. Why, that dead woman would by this time be nearly thirty years of age; whereas Miriam doesn't look two-and-twenty. Besides, the whole character and expression of her face are changed. There remain the same bony structure and the same general complexion: that is all that remains the same. Confess that the thing is impossible."

"When he saw her, he started and coloured up."

"Well, even so. What of it. He started and coloured up. What does that prove? Perhaps it was because of her resemblance to the dead woman, whom we will suppose him to have known. But as for identifying them as one and the same, he'd never dream of it. A merry, innocent young girl, of one or two-and-twenty, and a sad-eyed, sorrow-stricken, sinful woman, eight years her senior! The thing is on the face of it absurd. Absurd, too, is the supposition that he ever knew Louise Massarte at all. He started and coloured up at sight of Miriam, for the very simple reason of her exceeding beauty. He is a young man, and he is an artist. What quick-blooded young man, what artist, would not colour up at the sight of so beautiful a girl? Or else, it is imaginable, he has seen Miriam herself somewhere before—in the street, in an omnibus, or where not—and has been impressed by her loveliness; and then he started for surprise and pleasure at finding himself under the same roof with her. You, my good Josephine, you have jumped to a most unwarranted conclusion. Your fear was the father of your thought.— Afterwards, for instance? Did he follow up his start with such conduct as was calculated to justify you in your suspicion?"

"No. He simply returned our salutations, and behaved toward her as he did toward me—as if she were a perfectly new acquaintance."

"Good! And then, consider the freedom and the nonchalance with which he talked to her at luncheon. No, no; it is impossible. Well, I will keep an eye upon him during dinner. And when you and Miriam leave us to our cigars, I'll seek to find out what the true explanation of the matter may be."

And my sister and I descended to the drawing-room.

CHAPTER XI.
REASSURANCE.

Throughout the meal that followed, I carefully observed Fairchild's bearing toward my niece; and great was my satisfaction to see in it only and exactly what under the circumstances could rightly have been expected. Frank, gay, interested, attentive, yet undeviatingly courteous, respectful, and even deferential, it was precisely the bearing due from a young gentleman of good breeding toward the lady at whose side he found himself, and whose acquaintance he had but lately made.

"So that," I concluded, "of all conceivable theories adequate to account for his behaviour at first setting eyes upon her, Josephine's is the farthest-fetched and the least tenable."

For the matter of that, as I had assured my sister, I was confident that her own mother, had she been alive, must have failed to identify her, so essentially was she altered both in expression of countenance and in apparent age, to say nothing of her totally transformed personality. That Fair-child did not do so I was certain. His manner exhibited neither surprise, mystification, curiosity, nor constraint. It would have required a far cunninger hypocrite than I took him to be, so effectually to have disguised such emotions, had he really felt them; and he could not have helped feeling them if, having known the dead woman, Louise Massarte, he had recognised her in the young and unsophisticated maiden, Miriam Benary. The right theory by which to explain his conduct at first meeting her, I purposed discovering, if I could, when he and I were alone.

He and Miriam had a deal of fun together making the salad, in which enterprise they collaborated—not, however, without much laughing difference as to the best method of procedure. He pretended that, instead of rubbing the bowl with garlic, one should introduce a *chapon*—or crust of bread discreetly tinctured with that herb—and "fatigue" it with the lettuce: whereas our niece vigorously maintained the contrary. And finally they drew lots to determine which policy should prevail, Miriam winning.

"I am defeated but not disheartened," Fair-child declared. "If there is anything upon which I pride myself, Miss Benary, it is my erudition in the science, and my dexterity in the art, of gastronomy. You have taken it out of my power to display my skill in salad-making; but now, if you are a generous victor, you will give me an opportunity to distinguish myself in the confection of an omelet. It is an omelet of my own invention, a sort of cross between the ordinary *omelette-au-vin* of the French and the Italian *zabaiano*, I shall require the use of that chafing dish and spirit-lamp which I see yonder on the sideboard, the sherry decanter, and half a dozen eggs. I can promise your palates a delectable experience; and you, Miss Denary, by watching me, will acquire an invaluable talent."

So, with much merriment, he proceeded with the manufacture of his omelet, Miriam observing and assisting. When it was complete, we unanimously voted it the most delicious thing in the way of an omelet that we had ever tasted. But Miriam sighed, and said, "It is all very simple except the most important point. The way is toss it up into the air, and make it turn over, and then catch it again as it descends—I am sure I shall never be able to do that."

"Never? That is a long word. You must practise it with beans," said Fairchild. "A pint of beans—dry beans—the kind Bostonians use for baking. Three hours daily practice for six months, and you will do it almost as easily as I do."

After the fruit the ladies left us; and having filled our glasses and lighted our cigars, we sipped and smoked for a few minutes without speaking. Fairchild was the first to break the silence.

"I can do nothing," he began, "but congratulate myself upon the happy chance—if chance it was, and not a kind Providence—that brought about our encounter this morning. For once in my life I was in luck."

"It seems to me," I replied, "that it is I who was in luck, and who have the best occasion for self-gratulation."

"That would depend upon the dubious question of the value of life," said he. "Has it ever struck you that this earth of ours is, after all, only a huge grave-yard, a colossal burying-ground; and that we living persons are simply waiting about—standing in a long *queue*, so to speak—till our turn comes to be interred? That seems to me a very pleasing fancy, and one which, considered as an hypothesis, clarifies many obscure things. Accepting it, we cease to wonder at the phenomenon of death, and regard it as the chief end, aim, object, and purpose of all human life—the consummation devoutly to be wished, which we are all attending with greater or less impatience. Anyhow, I am sceptical whether we confer a boon or inflict a bane upon the human being whom we bring into existence, or whose exit therefrom we prevent. It is indeed probable that, except for our casual meeting this morning, you would at the present hour have been numbered among the honoured dead. But, very likely—either enjoying the excitements of the happy hunting-ground or sleeping the deep sleep of annihilation—very likely, I say, you would have been better off than you are actually, or can ever hope to be in the flesh. About my good fortune, contrariwise, debate is inadmissible. Here I am in veritable clover-smoking a capital cigar after a capital dinner, in capital company, to the accompaniment of a capital glass of wine, and the richer by the acquisition of three new friends—for as friends, I trust, I may be allowed to reckon you and your ladies. Had we not happened to run across each other in the way we did, on the other hand, I should now have been seated alone by my bachelor's hearth, with no companions more congenial to me than my plaster casts, and no voice more jovial to cheer my solitude than the howling of the gale."

"It is very flattering of you to put the matter as you do," said I; "but being modish in no respect, I am least of all so in my metaphysics. Therefore I cannot share your pessimistic doubt of the value of life; and I assure you I should have hated bitterly to leave mine behind me in that ungodly snowbank. It is true, I am perilously close to the Scriptural limitation of man's age; and I ought perhaps to feel that I have had my fit and proper share of this world's vanities, and to be prepared for my inevitable journey to the next. But, I must confess, I am so little of a philosopher, I should dearly like to tarry here a few years longer; and hence, I maintain, my obligation to you is indisputably established."

"Well, then, so far as I can see, we may say measure for measure; and consider ourselves quit."

"Hardly. The balance is still tremendously in your favour."

After that we again smoked for a while without speaking. Then again Fairchild broke the silence.

"I wonder whether you would take it amiss, Dr. Benary, if I should mention something which has been the object of my delighted admiration almost from the moment I entered your house?"

"Ah! What is that?" I queried.

"I fear you will condemn me as overbold if I answer you candidly; but I shall do so, and accept the consequences. The circumstance that I am an artist may be pleaded in my behalf, if I seem to transcend the bounds of the conventional."

"You pique my curiosity. What is it that you allude to? I do not think you need be apprehensive of my wrath. My extended 'Life of Sir Joshua'? That is the fruit of ten years' hard labour. Or my Japanese woman by Theodore Wores? It's a wonderful piece of flesh-painting. It looks as though it would bleed if you pricked it" *

"Yes, it is in Worcs's best vein. But that is not what I have in mind. Neither is the 'Life of Sir Joshua.' which, by-the-bye, I have not seen."

* *The Editor of this work must disclaim all responsibility*

Dr. Benary's opinions upon matters literary and aesthetic.

"Not seen it? Oh, well, I must show it to you directly we go upstairs. It's my particular pet and pride. But what, then? I do not know what else I have worthy of such admiration as you profess."

"You have—if you will tolerate my saying so—you have a niece; and I allude to her extraordinary beauty."

My pulse quickened. Here had he, of his own accord, broached that very topic upon which I was anxious to sound him.

"Ah, yes; Miriam," I assented, a trifle nervously, and wondering what would come next. "Miriam. Yes, Miriam is a very pretty girl."

"Pretty!" echoed he. "Pretty? Why, sir, she's—— why, in all my life I've not seen so beautiful a woman. And it isn't simply that she is so beautiful; it's her type. Her type—I believe I am conservative when I call it the least frequent, the rarest, in the whole range of womanhood. Forgive my fervour: I speak in my professional capacity—as an artist, as one to whom the beautiful is the subject-matter of his daily studies. It is a type of which you occasionally see a perfect specimen in antique marble, but in flesh and blood not oftener than once in a lifetime. To say nothing of her colouring, which a painter would go mad over, consider the sheer planes and lines of her countenance! That magnificent sweep of profile—brow, nose, lips, chin, and throat, described by one splendid flowing line! It's unutterable. It's Juno-esque. It's worth ten years of commonplaceness to have lived to see it in a veritable breathing woman."

"Yes," I admitted, "it's a fine profile—a noble face."

"Her type is so rare," he went on, "that, as I have said, Nature succeeds in producing a perfect specimen of it scarcely oftener than once in a generation. Of faulty specimens—comparable, from a sculptor's point of view, to flawed castings—she turns out many every year. You have been in Provence? In the Noonday of France? Arles, Tours, Avignon, teem with such failures— women who approach, approach, approach, but always fall short of, the perfection that your niece embodies."

"Yes, I know the Méridionales, and I see the resemblance that you refer to. But, as you intimate, they are coarse and crude copies of Miriam. That expression of high spirituality, which is the dominant note in her face, is usually quite absent from theirs."

"They compare to her as the pressed terracotta effigies of the Venus of Milo, which may be bought for a song in the streets, compare to the chiselled marble in the Louvre. In all my life I have never known but one woman who could properly be mentioned in the same breath with her. And even she was a good distance behind. Of her I happened to see just enough to perceive the divine potentiality of the type. Ever since, I have been watching for a faultless specimen. And to-day, when Miss Benary came into the room where you had left me, I declare for a moment my breath was taken away. I could scarcely believe my eyes. Such beauty seemed beyond reality; it was like a dream come true. In my admiration I forgot my manners: it was some seconds before I remembered to make my bow. The point of all which is that when our friendship is older, you, Dr. Benary, must permit *me* to model her portrait."

Thus was my mind set at ease.

Presently we rejoined the ladies, and while Fairchild and Miriam chatted together in the bow window, I drew Josephine aside, and communicated to her the upshot of our post-prandial conversation. She breathed a mighty sigh, and professed herself to be enormously relieved.

CHAPTER XII.
THE DOCTOR'S DILEMMA.

Fairchild became a frequent visitor at our house, and an ever-welcome one. His good looks, his good sense, his droll humour, his honesty, his high spirits, made him an extremely pleasant companion. We all liked him cordially; we were always glad to see him. I told him that if pot-luck had no terrors for him, he must feel at liberty to drop in and dine with us whenever his inclination prompted and his leisure would permit. He took me at my word, as I meant he should; and from that time forth he broke bread with us never seldomer than one evening out of the seven.

At the end of a month, or perhaps six weeks, Josephine said to me, "Do you think it well, Leonard, that two young people of opposite sexes should be thrown together as frequently and as closely as Mr. Fairchild and Miriam are?"

"Why not?" questioned I.

"The reasons are obvious. How would you be pleased if they should fall in love?"

"The Lord forbid! But I see no danger of their doing so."

"There is always danger when a beautiful young girl and a spirited young man see too much of each other."

"But Fairchild pays no more attention to Miriam than he does to you or to me. They are never left alone together. They are simply good friends."

"As yet, perhaps, yes. But time can change friendship into love. He begins, you must remember, with the liveliest and most profound admiration for her; she, with the deepest sense of gratitude towards him. True, as you say, they are never left alone together—not exactly alone, that is. But are they not virtually alone when you and I are seated here in the library over our backgammon-board, and he and she are therein the drawing-room at the piano?"

"But, my dear sister, the two rooms are as one. The folding doors are never closed."

"True again: we are all within sight and hearing of one another. But as a matter of fact, you and I give no heed to them, nor do they to us. There are certain laws of nature which should not be ignored."

"Well, what do you want me to do?" I enquired rather testily. "Shall I forbid Fairchild the house? Forbid my house to the man who saved my life?"

"Oh, no, of course not. You know I could not wish such a thing as that. Mr. Fairchild's claims upon our gratitude must never be forgotten. And besides, I like him, and I enjoy his visits as heartily as you do. Only——"

"Only what? If I don't forbid him the house, how can I prevent him and Miriam meeting? Shall I direct her to keep her room whenever he comes?"

"I do think, brother, it would be well if she were not always present when he comes. If you wish to hear my honest opinion, I believe it is to see her that he comes so often, and not to see a couple of sober, elderly folk like you and me. I cannot think that you and I are so irresistibly attractive as to draw him to our house as frequently as once or twice a week. However, I only wished to call your attention to the matter. It is for you now to act as your best judgment dictates."

"Well, then, my good Josephine, I shall not act at all. There is no occasion for my acting. I should be most unjust and unreasonable to prevent these two young people getting what innocent pleasure they can from each other's friendship and society, simply because in the abstract it is true that they are not incapable of falling in love. I might, as reasonably enjoin Miriam against ever going out of doors, because it is possible that in the street she might be run over; against ever drinking a glass of water, because it is possible that the water might contain a disease-germ. You have conjured up a chimera. Your fears are those of a too imaginative woman. When I perceive the first symptom of anything sentimental existing between them, it will be time enough to act."

"Perhaps then, Leonard, it will be too late," retorted Josephine, and with that she dropped the subject.

———

Well, of course, as the reader has foreseen, that very complication which my sister feared and warned me of, and which I refused to consider—of course that very complication came to pass. Fairchild fell in love with Miriam, and Miriam reciprocated his unfortunate passion. Otherwise his name would never have been introduced into this narrative; or, rather, there would have been no such narrative for me to recite.

In June, 1888, Josephine, Miriam, and I went down to the little village of Ogunquit, on the coast of Wade, there to rusticate until the autumn. Toward the end of July, Fairchild joined us there, pursuant to an arrangement made before we left town; and it was on the evening of the 15th of August that he requested a few minutes' private talk with me, and then informed me of the condition of affairs.

"I love your niece with all my heart and soul, Dr. Benary. Indeed, I have loved her from the day I first became acquainted with her—the day of that blessed Blizzard. I should like to know, who could help loving her: she is so good and so intelligent, to say nothing of her beauty. To-day I emptied my heart out to her, and she has made me the happiest man in Christendom by signifying her willingness to become my wife. So, now, it only remains for you to give us your approval and benediction. I have an income sufficient to keep the wolf from the door, over and above my earnings; and for the rest, you know me well enough to judge of my eligibility for yourself."

What answer could I give him?

Putting aside altogether, as I was bound to do, the selfish consideration that her marriage would deprive us of the treasure and the blessing of our old age, and leave our home desolate and forsaken—could I in honour, could I in justice to the man, permit him to make Miriam Benary his wife, without first imparting to him so much as I myself knew concerning Louise Massarte?

But the latter was a thing which, I was persuaded, I had no manner of right to do. The secret of her connection with Louise Massarte, Miriam herself was ignorant of. Surely, no other human being had the shadow of a claim to learn it Miriam Benary had never even heard of Louise Massarte. Louise Massarte was dead and abolished utterly. Therefore, to saddle Miriam, in her youth and her innocence, with that dead woman's name and history, to put upon her the burden of the dead woman's sin and shame, it would be to do her not only a most grievous, but a most unwarrantable, wrong.

No, I could not, I would not, I must not, tell Fairchild the story of Louise Massarte's annihilation, and the consequent existence of Miriam Benary. Yet how could I say, "Yes, you may marry her," and keep that story to myself? What excuse could I invent wherewith to ease my conscience, if I should practise such deceit upon him in an issue that involved his dearest and most vital interests? *Suppressio veri, suggestio falsi.* I should be as bad as any liar if I gave my consent to their marriage, while allowing him to remain in error respecting the truth about his bride—truth which, if made known to him, might radically modify his intentions.

But furthermore, and on the other hand, suppose I should say in reply to his demand, "No, you cannot marry her"—what right had I to say that? What reason could I allege in justification of my refusal? Not the actual reason; for that would be to tell him the very story which, I had made up my mind, I must not and should not tell. And if I alleged a fictitious reason, I should simply escape the devil to plunge into the deep sea—I should simply exchange a lie for a falsehood. These young people loved each other. Therefore, to set up impediments to their union, would be to impose upon each of them endless unmerited pain. What right had I to do that? It was a vexed and difficult quandary. There were strong arguments for and strong arguments against either course out of it.

"Well, Dr. Benary, you do not answer me," Fairchild said.

"I can't answer you. You must give me time—time to consider, to consult my sister, to make up my mind."

We had been strolling together, he and I, up and down the sands. Now we returned to the inn. Josephine was seated on the verandah, near the entrance.

"Ah, Leonard, at last!" she exclaimed, starting up the moment she caught sight of me. "I have been waiting for you."

I accompanied her to her room.

"Well," she began, as soon as the door was closed behind us, "the worst has happened, as I suppose you know. Mr. Fairchild has spoken to you, has he not?"

"Ah! Then you, too, know about it?" queried I.

"Miriam has just told me the whole story."

"What does she say?"

"That Mr. Fairchild has asked her to be his wife; that she loves him, and has accepted him—conditionally, that is, upon your approval."

"She says she loves him?"

"She says she loves him with all her heart. She says she is as happy as the day is long. She doesn't dream that you will have any hesitation about consenting."

For a little while we were silent. At last, "Well, what are you going to do?" my sister asked.

"That is what I wish to advise with you about."

"Have you given any answer to Mr. Fair-child?"

"I have said to him that I must take time for reflection, and for consultation with you."

"Well?"

"Well, it is a most difficult dilemma."

"But you have got to make up your mind, one way or the other; and that speedily. It is cruel to keep them in suspense."

"I know that, my dear sister."

"Do you mean to say yes or no?"

"That's just it. That's just the difficulty, isn't it?"

"But it is a difficulty which must be solved. You will have to say one of the two."

"How dare I say yes?"

"They love each other."

"What right have I to say no?"

"It is their life-happiness which is at stake."

"Exactly, exactly; therefore, if I say no, it will be to condemn them both to great misery, and misery which they have done nothing to deserve."

"It certainly will—it will break Miriam's heart. And what reason can you give them for saying no? It will seem all the harder to them, because it will seem so unreasonable and unnecessary, so unjustifiable and wanton. They will feel that it is an act of wilful cruelty, on the part of a selfish, tyrannical old man."

"I know it, I know it," I groaned. "And yet, on the other hand, if I say yes——"

"If you say yes, you will assure to them the greatest happiness their hearts can desire."

"But how dare I say yes without sharing with Fairchild the secret of Miriam's origin? Without telling him the story of Louise Massarte?"

"Surely, you cannot purpose doing that! You cannot mean to confide to another knowledge affecting her which she herself is unaware of!"

"No, of course not. But there's just the rub. How, without doing that, how can I honourably permit him to make her his wife?"

"It is a choice of evils: to break their hearts or to suppress certain facts. You must choose the lesser evil of the two."

"That is very easily said. But the trouble is to determine which of the two evils *is* the lesser. Deceit or cruelty?"

"Forgive me, my dear brother, for reminding you of it: but if you had listened to my warning in the first place, this painful alternative would never have come about."

"What could I do? You yourself agreed with me that I couldn't forbid Fairchild the house. And so long as he had the run of the house, how could I prevent him and Miriam meeting? And meeting as frequently as they did, I suppose it was inevitable that they should come to love each other. There's no use reproaching me—no use regretting the past. What was bound to happen has happened. That's the whole truth of it."

"I did not intend to reproach you, Leonard. I merely wished to say that, since, in a manner, you have been responsible for the state of things which has come to pass—since, in other words, you neglected to take such measures as would have prevented that state of things from coming to pass—it seems as if now you were under a sort of moral obligation not to stand between them and their happiness. The time for action was the outset. You did not act then. It seems as if you had thereby forfeited your right to act. Since you have allowed things to go so far, it seems as if you had no right to forbid their going farther."

"That is to say, you counsel me to consent."

"*I* do not see how you can do otherwise now. It is too late for you to step in and separate them."

"And the point of honour? I am to suppress the truth? I am to stand still and suffer Fair-child to make Miriam his wife, in ignorance of certain facts which, if he were aware of them, might totally change his feeling? How can I do that? It would lie for ever on my conscience."

"So far from totally changing his feeling I do not believe those facts, if Fairchild knew them, would weigh with him so much as one hair's weight. They would not, if his love for Miriam is love in any vital sense of the word. He would agree with us in looking upon her as an entirely different person from Louise Massarte. However, he must not know, he must not even dream those facts. Therefore, as I said before, it is a choice of evils. The negative evil of suppressing the truth does not seem to me so great as the positive evil of inflicting pain. Besides, after all, is it not Miriam's prerogative to decide this matter for herself? What right have you or I to do anything but stand aside, with hands off, and let her choose her husband without constraint or interference? She is of full age and sound mind; and our relationship with her, which would give us our pretence for interfering, is, as you know, only a fiction She could not wish for a better husband than Mr. Fairchild. No woman could."

"What you say, my dear Josephine, and what you suggest, are Jesuitry, pure and simple."

"There come emergencies in which Jesuitry is the only feasible policy."

A long silence followed. In the end, "Where is Miriam now?" I asked.

"She was in her room when I left her."

"Will you find her, and send her to me? Or rather, bring her. You must be present, too, to lend me countenance—to give me moral support in the grossly immoral action which I am going to perpetrate. I feel like a pickpocket. I need the encouragement of my accomplice."

Josephine went off. In three minutes she returned, leading Miriam by the hand.

Miriam's cheeks and throat turned crimson as she saw me; and she dropped her eyes, and stood still, waiting.

"My dear——" I called, holding out my hands.

She came to me, and put her arms around my neck, and buried her face upon my shoulder.

"So this young rascal of a sculptor has asked you to be his wife?" I began.

"Yes," she murmured, scarcely louder than a whisper.

"And so—the double-faced rogue!—it was not, as we had supposed, because of his great fondness for your aunt and uncle, that he became a frequenter of our camp, but because he had covetous designs upon our chief treasure!"

"Oh! but he is very fond of my aunt and uncle, too," she protested.

"Is he, indeed! Well, what answer have you given him?"

"I said—I said I—I said I liked him."

"Ah! I see. You said you liked him. That was rather irrelevant, wasn't it?—a little evasive? He asked you to become his wife, and you said you liked him. Did you give him no more categorical an answer than that?"

"I said he must ask you."

"Ask me? Ask me what? It isn't I that he wants to marry. And I wouldn't have him, anyhow. Why should he ask me?"

"You know what I mean. I told him I could not marry without your consent."

"And suppose I should withhold my consent?"

"I should be very unhappy."

"But I don't really see what my consent matters. It's for you to decide. You're of full age. I have no right to forbid you. Now, then, what are you going to do?"

"I said I would be his wife, unless you wished otherwise."

"Well, I suppose you must keep your word. The poor fellow is waiting on the anxious seat to learn his fate. I really think, instead of tarrying here, you ought to seek him out, and put an end to his suspense."

She hugged me and kissed me, and said some very jubilant and some very complimentary things; and then she began to cry, and then she laughed through her tears; and at last she went off to find her lover, and to convey to him the joyful tidings.

They were married on the 15th day of December, and that same afternoon they set sail for Havre aboard the steamship *La Touraine*, to pass six months abroad. Anxiously did Josephine and I count the days that must elapse before the post would bring us their first letter; and little did we dream what ominous news that letter would contain.

CHAPTER XIII.
NATURE BEGINS REPRISALS.

OF course, we watched the newspapers for an announcement of the *Touraine's* arrival. A fast steamer, ordinarily accomplishing the passage within seven days, she ought to have reached Havre on the 22nd. She was not reported, however, until Monday, the 24th, being then two days overdue.

It was on Friday, the 4th of January, that we at last got a letter. The envelope was superscribed not in Miriam's band, but in Fairchild's; and when we tore it open we saw that the letter itself had been written by the groom, and not by the bride. This struck us as rather odd, and made us a little uneasy. We hastened to read:

"Hôtel de la Grande Bretagne,

"Havre, December 25.

"Dear Dr. Benary,

"Christmas day, and such news as I have to give you! I should put off writing until we reach Paris, in the hope that when we are there the face of things may have altered for the better; only I know, if you don't receive a letter sooner than you would in that case, you will be alarmed.

"What I have to tell you is so horrible in itself, it must shock you dreadfully whatever way I put it. I can't hope to make it any less painful for you by mincing it, or beating about the bush. Yet it seems brutal to state the hideous fact downright. Miriam has become blind, totally blind.

"Whether incurably so or not, we do not yet know. Of course we hope for the best, but we can be sure of nothing till we reach Paris, where we shall consult the best oculists to be found. Meantime, you may imagine our state of mind.

"We had a most frightful passage, and that was the cause of it. We ran into a storm directly we left Cape Thunderhead; and it followed us all the way across. Bad enough at the outset, it got steadily worse and worse until we reached port. It had only this mitigation—it was behind us, and moved in the same direction with us. Therefore we were delayed but about forty-eight hours. If it had been against us, there's no telling when we should have got ashore; and twenty-four hours more of it Miriam could never have survived.

"For six consecutive days (from the 17th to the 23rd) the hatches were battened down; no passengers were allowed on deck; and not only were the port-holes kept permanently closed, but the inner iron shutters were screwed up, lest the sea should break in and swamp us. The skylights also were, covered. Thus daylight was excluded, as well as fresh air. Then the electric-lighting machine got out of order, and we had to fall back upon candles and petroleum. The atmosphere in the cabins became something unendurable. Much of the time, owing to the violent motion, it was impossible to keep even the candles or the petroleum lamps burning; and we were condemned to total darkness. At last, however, they got the electric machine into running gear again, so that we had light. From second to second, day and night, the sea broke over us with a roar like the discharge of cannon, making every timber of the ship creak and tremble. It was enough to drive one frantic, that everlasting rhythmic thunder.

"And all the while we were tossed up, down, and around, as if that giant vessel were a cockle-shell. Standing erect or walking was not to be thought of. I had to creep from place to place on hands and knees. And then the never-ending motion, and the incessant noise: the howling of the wind, the pounding of the water, the creaking of timbers, the snapping of cordage, the clanking of chains, the crashing of loose things being knocked about, the shouts and tramping of sailors overhead, the groans of sea-sick people, the shrieks of scared women and children, the darkness, the loathsome air—I tell you it was frightful; it was like pandemonium gone mad; the memory of it is like the memory of a nightmare.

"Miriam suffered excruciatingly from seasickness. It was the most heart-rending sight I have ever witnessed, the agony she endured. I had never dreamed that sea-sickness could be so terrible; and the ship's surgeon said he had never seen so severe a case. What made it worse, of course, was the hopelessness of her obtaining any relief until the storm abated, or until we reached shore. There was nothing anyone could do. I just sat there beside her, and held her hand, while she either lay exhausted, or started up and went through the torments of the damned. I can give you no idea of what she suffered. It was hard work to sit still there, and watch her sufferings, and realise that I was utterly powerless to help her in any way. From Monday, the 17th, until last night, when we had been ashore some hours—precisely one week—she did not taste food. Once in a while she would drink a little water, with a drop of brandy in it; but even that distressed her cruelly. On the 20th she was seized with convulsions, awful beyond description. From then on, until we left the ship, she simply alternated between terrible paroxysms and utter prostration. Four days! I thought she was going to die, her convulsions were so violent, the prostration that ensued was so death-like. The ship's surgeon himself admitted that there was great danger—that death might result from exhaustion. For those four days—from the 20th to the 24th—he kept her almost constantly under the influence of opiates. On Saturday she seemed a little better—that is, her convulsions occurred seldomer, and were of shorter duration. When not in convulsions, she would lie in a stupor, as if asleep, only most of the time her eyes were half open, and she would groan. But on Sunday she was worse again; and it was on Sunday night, about ten o'clock, that, after she had lain perfectly quiet for an hour or so, all at once she started up, and asked me whether the electric lights had gone out again. The lights were at that moment burning brightly in our state-room; and I told her so. Then she cried: 'I can't see you. I can't see anything. It is all dark. What has happened? I believe I am blind.'

"Of course, I thought it must be some hallucination caused by her sickness. I could not believe that she had really become blind. But the ship's surgeon came and made an examination, and discovered that it was so. He could attribute it only to a paralysis of the optic nerve, the consequence of shock and exhaustion. What the danger of its being permanent was he could not say.

"Yesterday, thank God, that hellish voyage came to an end. The instant we reached this hotel, I got her into bed and sent off for the best medical men this town holds. They simply corroborated the judgment of the ship's doctor—that she is suffering from shock and exhaustion, and that her blindness is due to a paralysis of the optic nerve. *They think it will probably not be permanent.* She must keep her bed until she is thoroughly rested, which will take several days. Then we must go to Paris, and put her under the treatment of Dr. Geoffroy Désessaires, who, it seems, is the great French specialist in diseases of the eye.

"She is in bed now, in the next room, sleeping. She sleeps most of the time— or rather, dozes. Her convulsions are over now, I hope for good. But all last night they occurred from time to time—very much less violently, however, than when on ship-board. She has not yet been able to take much nourishment, but as often as she wakes, I give her a little beef-tea.

"That is about all there is to tell down to the present moment. You will understand that I am in no condition of mind to write at greater length than is necessary, having gone without sleep for the greater part of a week, to say nothing of anxiety and distress. When she wakes she talks of you and bids me say how she loves you. And of course you always means yourself and Miss Josephine.

"I pray God that in my next letter I may have more cheering news to write.

"Always yours,

"Henry Fairchild."

The dismay which the foregoing epistle occasioned Josephine and myself the sympathetic reader will conceive without my telling. But it was as nothing to that which we experienced when we read the next, and considered its purport:—

"Hôtel de la Bourdonnaye,

"Paris, January 1, 1889.

"Dear Dr. Benary,

"Miriam improved rapidly after I posted my letter of Christmas day. Rest, quiet, and nourishment were what she needed—and those she had. The doctors gave us permission to leave Havre yesterday; and we arrived here in the afternoon. She is pale and weak, and wasted to the merest shadow of herself, having lost *twenty-six pounds* in weight. But she does not suffer any more bodily pain; though what her agony of mind must be it is not difficult for those who love her to imagine. However, that will soon be over.

"I telegraphed in advance to Dr. Désessaires, requesting him to call upon us here at our hotel last evening. He came at eight o'clock, and put Miriam through a thorough examination. He confirmed what all the other doctors had said—that it was a paralysis of the optic nerve. He enquired all about her health in the past, and particularly whether she had ever had any trouble of the brain or spine. Then, of course, we told him of that accident which she met with in 1884, which had deprived her of her memory, 'Ah! said he, 'that gives me the key to the whole difficulty.' He proceeded very carefully to examine her head, and when he had finished he said there was a depression of the bone at the point where she had been hurt at that time, and a consequent pressure upon the brain; and it was that pressure upon the brain which accounted for the extraordinary violence of her sea-sickness and the resultant blindness. Finally, he said that an operation to relieve that pressure would, if made at once, restore her sight; but that, unless such an operation was performed, she must remain permanently blind. He assured me that the operation was not a dangerous one; that it would consist in the removal of a minute fragment of the bone—what is called trephining. Of course, there was nothing for us to do but consent to having the operation performed; and thereupon he went away, saying he would return this morning.

"At eleven o'clock this morning he arrived, accompanied by four other physicians—Dr. Cidolt, also an oculist; Dr. Gouet, the famous alienist; Dr. Marsac, a general practitioner of very high standing; and Dr. Larquot, said to be the most skilful surgeon in France. They made a long examination, and then withdrew to consult together. At the end of nearly two hours they came to me with their report, which was simply a repetition of what Dr. Dêsessaires had already said—that trephining would be necessary, that it would be effective, and that it would be as free from danger as such an operation ever is. It must be performed as soon as possible, so that atrophy of the optic nerve may not have time to set in; but before they can safely undertake it, Miriam must be perfectly recovered in general health. They have set upon this day fortnight—the 14th—as probably a favourable time. Meanwhile she is under the care of Dr. Marsac. Dr. Larquot is to conduct the operation.

"The brave little woman! She supports her calamity so patiently! And she looks forward to that dreadful ordeal with an amount of nerve and courage that a man might be proud of. God grant that all may go well.

"There is nothing more for me to write at present.

"Always Yours,

"Henry Fairchild."

At the close of Fairchild's letter this postscript was added, in a hand that we recognised as Miriam's, though it was cramped and irregular, as if she had written with her eyes shut:—

"Dear Ones,—I cannot see to write to you; but I love you and love you, with all my heart.

"Miriam."

When my sister Josephine read that, she burst out crying like a child.

I waited till she had dried her tears. Then, "Well, my dear sister," I questioned, "do you realise what that letter means?"

"What it means? Why, that her blindness is only temporary, and can be cured. That she will recover her sight."

"Nothing else?"

"What else?"

"What else! This else—and I am surprised that you do not see it for yourself—it means that the same operation which will restore her sight will also restore her memory. Do you understand? She will become Louise Massarte again. She will begin at the precise point where Louise Massarte left off. She will forget everything that has occurred during the past four years, and will recall what occurred before. It is that same pressure of the bone upon the brain to which they rightly or wrongly attribute her blindness—it is that same pressure of the bone upon the brain which keeps Louise Massarte in quiescence, and makes Miriam Benary possible. Relieve that pressure, remove that point of bone, and instantly Louise Massarte will spring into life again, while at the same moment Miriam Benary will cease to exist. That is what Fairchild's letter means."

"Good Heavens!" gasped Josephine, holding up her hands in helpless dismay. "But—but surely—— but what—what is to be done?"

"Which, in your opinion, would be the lesser of the two evils—to have her remain permanently blind, or to have her regain her memory? She would recollect all that she is happiest in forgetting, she would forget all that she is happiest in remembering. The four years during which she has lived here with us as our niece would be utterly obliterated and undone. She would rise from that operation in mind and spirit exactly where she was, and exactly what she was, just before you and I put her under the influence of ether on the 14th day of June, 1884. Which, I want you to tell me—which would be the lesser evil: the blindness of Miriam Benary, or the resurrection of Louise Massarte?"

"Oh, there is no room for question about that. Better a thousand times that she should never see the light of day again, than that she should cease to be herself, and return to her dead personality. Why, it is—it is Miriam's very life, her very existence, which is at stake."

"Precisely. It is, so far as she is concerned, a choice between blindness and death. Nay, something worse than death: a hideous transformation of her identity, from that of a pure and innocent young bride, to that of a weary, heart-sick, sinful woman-convict. To cure her blindness by the means which they propose, would simply be to kill her; to abolish Miriam Benary and to substitute for her Louise Massarte. It is infinitely better that she should remain blind. Therefore, I am going to prevent that operation if I can."

"If you can indeed! But how can you? They are three thousand miles away. How can you?"

"Well, let us see. To-day—to-day is the 12th, is it not?"

"Yes, to-day is Saturday the 12th. Well?"

"Well, the day set for the operation is the 14th—that is, the day after to-morrow, Monday."

"Yes."

"Well, I shall go at once and cable to Fairchild, imploring him, commanding him, no matter at what cost, to postpone the operation until I arrive in Paris. Then I shall engage passage aboard the first swift steamer that sails. The South German Clyde steamers sail on Mondays. They make the passage in seven days, and touch at Cherbourg. Do you, meanwhile, prepare my things, so that I may take ship day after tomorrow. Once arrived in Paris, I will persuade Fairchild to relinquish the idea of the operation for good and all. I will convince him that Miriam's life will be imperilled. Or, failing in that, I may find myself compelled to tell him the truth about Louise Massarte. Anything will be better than to have her regain her memory."

"Yes, anything. God grant that he may not disobey your telegram. But you must engage passage for me as well as for yourself. I cannot stay at home here idle. You must let me go with you. I should die of anxiety alone here at home."

I went to the nearest telegraph office, and sent the following cable despatch:—

"Fairchild, Hôtel Bourdonnaye, Paris.

"At all costs postpone operation till I arrive. Miriam's life endangered. Sail Monday, viâ Cherbourg.

"Benary."

Then I hastened to the steamship company's office in Bowling Slip, and engaged staterooms for my sister and myself aboard the *Egmont* which was to sail promptly at noon on Monday the 14th.

Yet, despite these precautionary measures, a heavy load of anxiety lay upon my heart. What if Fairchild should suffer the operation to proceed, notwithstanding my protest? I could not banish that contingency from my mind, nor its ghastly *corollaries* from my imagination.

CHAPTER XIV.
ALTER EGO.

Though by no means so stormy as that described by Fairchild, our voyage was an unconscionably long one. To say nothing of fogs and head winds, an accident befell our machinery, whereby we were compelled to lie to for sixteen precious hours, while the damage was repaired. We did not make Cherbourg till the afternoon of Friday, January 25.

Ashore, my first act was to enquire when a train would leave for Paris. A train would leave at midnight, due at the capital at half past nine in the morning. My next act was to telegraph Fairchild, informing him of our arrival, and warning him to expect us on the morrow.

At half past nine to the minute, Saturday, we drew into the Gare St. Lazare. We were a little surprised not to find Fairchild there to meet us, and perhaps also a little disturbed. Was Miriam so ill that he dared not leave her? After seeing our luggage through the Customs House, we got into a cab, and were driven to the Hôtel de la Bourdonnaye.

I inquired for Mr. Fairchild.

"Monsieur Fairchild is in his room, Monsieur."

"Show us thither at once," said I.

"Pardon, Monsieur. If Monsieur will have the goodness to send up his card——"

"Josephine," I exclaimed, "how do you account for this? Apparently we are not expected. He does not meet us at the railway station; and here at his hotel we are required to send up our card."

"Well, send it up. We shall soon have an explanation," Josephine said; and I acted upon her advice.

In two minutes Fairchild appeared.

"What! Arrived!" he cried, seizing each of us by a band. "Your steamer was overdue; when did you get in? Why didn't you telegraph from Cherbourg?"

"Why *didn't* I telegraph? But I did. Do you mean to say you haven't received my despatch?"

"Not the ghost of one. If I'd known you were coming this morning—— But wait."

He stepped into the office of the hotel. Issuing thence in a moment, "There!" he cried, exhibiting a blue envelope, "here's your telegram. In America I should have received it twelve hours ago. But they manage these things better in France. It came last night, after I'd gone to bed and the authorities of this hostelery were too considerate to wake me. Then this morning, they say, they thought I was so much occupied that, they would do best to wait about delivering it till I was at leisure. That's French courtesy with a vengeance. However, you're safely arrived at last, and that's the important thing."

"And Miriam? Miriam?" I demanded impatiently.

"The doctors are with her even now," he answered.

"You got my cable despatch, of course, and put off the operation?"

"Yes, I got your despatch; and we put off the operation until all the physicians insisted that it must not be put off longer—that, if put off longer, it would be ineffective."

Panic-stricken, "You don't mean to say," I gasped, "you can't mean to say that it has been performed!"

"As I just told you, they're with her now. They are performing it at this moment?"

"Heavens and earth, man! Didn't I say in my telegram that it would imperil her life? Didn't I entreat you at all costs to postpone it until I arrived?"

"You did, certainly. But these other medical men, who were on the spot, and could examine her for themselves, were of one mind in declaring that her life would not be imperilled, but that the longer the operation was delayed, the greater would be the danger of atrophy of the optic nerve. Finally, on Wednesday of this week, they fixed upon this morning as the furthest date to which they could consent to postpone it. It was a choice between going on without your presence, and taking the risk of permanent blindness. So I had to let them proceed."

"You don't know what you have done! You have done that which you will repent to your dying day!!" I groaned, wringing my hands. "You might have known that I never should have telegraphed as I did—that I never should have packed up and taken ship for Europe at two days notice—unless it was a matter of life and death But where are they? Take me to them. Perhaps it is not yet too late. Perhaps I am still in time to prevent it. Take me to them at once.

"I doubt whether they will admit you. They would not allow me to be present, and I am her husband. I have had to walk up and down the corridor, waiting."

"Not admit me! They will admit me, if have to break down the door. Take me to them this instant."

"Very well," he assented. "This way."

He led me up a flight of stairs, and halted before a door, upon which he gently rapped.

The door was immediately opened by an elderly man, in professional broadcloth, who said in French: "You may enter now. It is finished."

My heart turned to ice. For a breathing-space I could neither move nor speak.

At last, with the stolidity that is born of despair, "Finished!" I repeated. "You have then trephined?"

"We have."

"And the patient——?"

"She is not yet recovered from the anaesthetic."

We entered the room. Miriam, pale and beautiful, lay unconscious upon a sofa near the windows. Two other professional-looking gentlemen stood over her, one of whom was fanning her face.

Fairchild presented me: "The English physician, Dr. Benary, the uncle of my wife."

I was in no mood to be courteous or ceremonious. Having bowed, "Gentlemen, I must beg you to leave me alone with the patient," I began, addressing the company at large.

My remark created a sensation. The French physicians exchanged perplexed and astonished glances; and a chorus of indignant "Mais, monsieurs," rose about my ears.

"Fairchild, I am in earnest," I said. "I insist upon these gentlemen leaving me alone with my niece. I look to you to see that they do so. I have neither the leisure nor the inclination to discuss the matter. Every second is precious." Somehow or other Fairchild prevailed upon them to withdraw. I suspect they saw that I was in no frame of mind to bear trifling with.

"I may remain?" Fairchild queried.

"No, not even you. I must be quite alone with her for the present."

"But——"

"Nay, do not waste time is controversy. Leave me at once."

Fairchild reluctantly went off.

I sat down at the side of Miriam's couch, and fanned her.

By-and-by she opened her eyes, and they rested upon my face.

From their expression, it was obvious that she saw me. Her blindness had been cured.

Almost at once, however, she closed her eyes again; and then for a little while she lay still, like one half asleep.

Suddenly she drew a deep quick breath, sat up, and looking me intently in the face, "Well, is it over?" she asked.

"Yes, dear; it is over," I replied. "Well, then, it is a failure—a total, abject failure! I remember everything. My memory was never clearer or more circumstantial. And you—you said there was no chance of failure! Oh, I was a fool to believe you. But what were you, to tell me such monstrous lies?"

With these words, she sighed, and fell back upon her pillow, while I, with a deadly sickness at the heart, realised that the worst which I had feared had come to pass.

She was Louise Massarte now. Where was Miriam Benary? She was Louise Massarte. She had taken up her former life at the exact point where Louise Massarte had dropped it. She had begun anew at the exact point where Louise Massarte had left off. And the operation which she had in her mind when she asked, "Is it over?" was the operation which I had performed upon her nearly five years before. Those intervening years were as perfectly erased from her consciousness as if they had been passed in dreamless sleep.

Where was Miriam Benary? What had become of that sweet and winning personality? And of the innocent pure love with which she had blessed our lives? Oh, it was a hideous transformation. Miriam was gone into the infinite void of Nothingness, leaving this changeling in her place. It was more unbelievable, it was more horribly impossible, than any wild nightmare phantasy, than any ancient grisly tale of necromancy; and yet it was true, it was undeniable, it was irremediable. It was worse, incomparably worse, than it would have been if she had died. For had she died, we could at least have hoped that her soul still lived, good and true and beautiful as ever. But now her soul had simply changed its form, and become the corrupt and sinful essence of Louise Massarte—just as in books of the Black Art we read of the fair virgin Princess being changed at a touch into a wicked grinning ape.

"Yes, you have failed, you have failed," she said again.

Then, all at once, starting up, and speaking passionately: "Oh, why did you interfere with me last night? Why did you cross my path and thwart my will? Why did you not let me die then, when it would have been so easy? Why did you bring me here to your house, to fill me and intoxicate me with hopes that were doomed to be disappointed? Oh, it was cruel, it was cruel of you. I was insane to listen to you. I was mad to place any sort of credence in what you said. It was so obvious a fairy-tale. I ought to have known that you promised the impossible, that you were either a liar or a lunatic.—But it is not yet too late. Leave me. Leave the room. Let me get up and dress myself, and go away. Where is your sister? She put away my clothes. Send her to me. I will not be detained here longer. Give me my clothes. I will get up, and go away, and throw myself into the river, before they have a chance to retake me, and send me back to prison."

What could I do? What could I say? "Oh, Miriam, Miriam," I faltered helplessly. "Calm yourself. For Heaven's sake, lie quiet. You will work yourself into a fever, into delirium. Your agitation may cost you your life. Lie quiet and let me think. My poor wits are distracted."

She caught at the name Miriam.

"Miriam? Miriam! Who is Miriam? Have I not told you my name? My name is Louise Massarte. Why do you call me by another? Miriam!—Miriam! Am I in a madhouse? *Oh, oh! my head!*" she screamed sharply, putting her hand to her head. "What have you done to my head? What have you done to me? Oh, I had such a pain! It shot through my head. Oh! fool, imbecile, that I was, ever to enter your house."

At this juncture the door opened, and Fair-child came into the room.

"I could wait outside no longer," he explained. "I heard her scream. I cannot stay away from her."

To my unspeakable amazement, she, at the sight of her husband (whom, I had every reason to suppose, she would not recognise), started violently, and, catching her breath, exclaimed—

"What! You! Henry Fairchild! Henry Fairchild! Here! Good God!"

"Yes, dear Miriam," Fairchild answered, coming forward, and putting out his hand to take hold of hers.

But she drew quickly away from him.

"Miriam again! Miriam! What farce is this? Am I really in a mad-house? Or have I gone mad? I believe you are both maniacs, that you call me Miriam. Or is it some charade that you are acting for my bewilderment? And you, Henry Fairchild! What are you doing here? You, of all men! Oh! this is some frightful trick that has been played upon me! This glib-tongued old man, with his innocent face and his protestations of benevolence, has trapped me here to send me back across the river. But why so much ceremony about it. Call your officers at once, and give me up to them. One thing I'll promise you: they'll never get me back there alive. Ha-ha-ha-ha-ha! And so, Mr. Fairchild, your friend, Roger Beecham, is dead. I came to town last night for the especial purpose of calling upon him, and settling our accounts; and then I learned that he had died from natural causes. Well, there is one consolation: unless the dogma of hell be a pure invention, he is roasting there now. I daresay I shall join him there presently, and then we will roast together! What a blow his death must have been to you, his faithful Achates!" During the first part of her speech, it was plain that poor Fairchild simply fancied her to be raving in delirium; but when she mentioned that name, Roger Beecham, an expression of terrified amazement, mingled with blank incomprehension, fell upon his face, and he stood staring at her, with knitted brows and parted lips, like a man dumbfoundered and aghast.

"Oh, I hope he died hard!" she cried. "I hope his mortal agony was excruciating and long-drawn out. I hope his death-bed was haunted and surrounded by twenty thousand hateful memories!" Fairchild found his tongue.

"Roger Beecham," he repeated, as if dazed. "What do you know of Roger Beecham?"

"That's good! That's exquisite!" cried she. "What do I know of Roger Beecham? You play your comedy very well, though I confess I don't see the point of it. What does Louise Massarte know of Roger Beecham? What does she *not* know of him?"

Fairchild became rigid.

"Louise Massarte!" he gasped. "What have you to do with Louise Massarte?—the murderess of Beecham's wife! Was she—for God's sake, was she related to you? Long ago I noticed a certain resemblance—a certain remote resemblance—such a resemblance as might exist between an angel and a devil. But why do you speak to me of her? What can you know of her? Louise Massarte!—— Dr. Benary, what has happened to my wife? She is delirious. Yet how comes she to know these names? What can be done?"

"I am not delirious, Mr. Fairchild," she put in, hastily. "But either you are, or you are a most clever actor, and have missed your vocation in failing to go upon the stage. As I said before, I cannot see the point of your mummery; but you do it uncommonly well. Why do you pretend not to recognise me? Surely, I can't have changed beyond recognition in two years."

"Not recognise you? Not recognise you, Miriam, my wife! Oh, what dreadful insanity has come upon her?"

"I? Miriam? Your wife?" She laughed. "Come, Mr. Fairchild, a truce to this mystery."

Fairchild sank upon a chair, and pressed his brow between his hands. "She is out of her senses. But how comes she to know those names?" he said, as if speaking to himself. Then, turning to me: "Perhaps you, Dr. Benary, can clear this puzzle up?"

"This is hardly a fitting time or place for attempting to," I replied. "If you had only respected my desires, there would have been no such occasion."

"Will you answer me this one question? Do you understand what she means by her reference to Louise Massarte?"

"Yes. I do."

"Explain that meaning to me."

"Not now, Fairchild. Not now. Later I will tell you everything. I have not the heart nor the wit to explain anything just now."

"But the relation, the connection, between that woman and my wife? Were they sisters?"

"No, not sisters."

"What then?"

"Fairchild, I implore you——" I began, but I got no further.

From the couch upon which Miriam lay came a low peal of sarcastic laughter. Then suddenly it expired in a most piteous moan. She gave a sharp cry, and swooned.

Fairchild was at her side in a twinkling. He knelt there, seizing her hands, and gazing with wild eyes into her face.

"She is dead! She is dead!" he groaned frantically.

"No, she has only fainted, from pain and exhaustion. But the consequences of a fainting fit in her condition may be terrible," said I.

"Oh, my darling! my darling!" he sobbed, bending over till his cheek swept her breast.

She never regained consciousness.

I have not the heart to dwell upon what followed.

This paragraph, cut from *Galignant's Messenger* of February 1, tells its own story:—

"*Fairchild.—On Wednesday morning, January 30, at the Hôtel de la Bourdonnaye, of phrenitis, Miriam Benary, wife of Henry Fairchild, of Adironda.*"

THE END.

Milton Keynes UK
Ingram Content Group UK Ltd.
UKHW030851011224
451361UK00001B/117

9 789362 928658